STREET KNOWLEDGE PUBLISHING

Published by: Street Knowledge Publishing

Street Knowledge Publishing
P.O. Box 345
Wilmington, DE 19899

I0525177

Copyright date: 2016
ISBN: 978-1-944151-26-3

Street Victims by Garry Haile
Edited by Navimjan Services LLC
Cover design by Street Knowledge Publishing Services
Formatted by Krystol Diggs
Typed from handwriting to text by Vanessa Cooper

www.streetknowledgepublishing.com

Printed in Canada

WORDS FROM THE AUTHOR

This is a story that many of us can relate to. Some of us chose this lifestyle, while others were forced upon this lifestyle. Some made it out, and some of us never had a chance. There's characters in this book that each individual reader can relate to. And if you can't relate, then you know someone who it reminds you of. Come into my world, where anybody at any time can fall victim to the streets. You're going to love this one. ENJOY!

GONE BUT NEVER FORGOTTEN

(Cameron Hamlin aka BLAZE)

&

(LORIAN HILL)

STREET VICTIMS

The city of Wilmington - a small city, is filled with people who have big dreams. Nothing is out of reach. Tre and his crew prove that they're a force to be reckoned with as they take you through the hazardous streets of Wilmington, Delaware and beyond, trying to make all of their dreams come true.

Casina - a beautiful woman from Miami, Florida who is searching for love; But her over-protective twin brothers will not allow her to have a love life. Desperately needing a get-away, she travels up north with her girlfriend where she encounters the man of her dreams, 'TRE'. Unknowingly to her, Tre has secrets...secrets that could cost him to his life and the girl of his dreams. Will Tre prevail? Or will he be yet another hood legend that falls victim to the streets?

CHAPTER 1: TRYING TO CATCH ME SLIPPIN'

With the AC on full blast and his left hand navigating the steering wheel; Tremane Money, known as "Tre" by many, bobbed to the lyrics of a local rapper, "Cazzy J." Heat wave records were being broken today; even at the close of day the city was still being attacked. The heat was unendurable. Yet, many still flocked and ambled up and down both sides of the street. Tre parted his index and middle finger to throw up deuces to a few individuals he knew. His black shiny car now sat at a traffic light on one of the most popular streets in the city of Wilmington, Delaware...Market Street. The polished rims of his car caught three young goons' attention. He glanced over the rim of his designer frames and observed the trio. The grimace on their face told it all.

"If these niggas had any fuckin sense, they'd go over to Rita's and cop them some water-ice," Tre whispered to himself. Rita's was located on Market Street. Locals from all over came to enjoy the best water-ice in the city. Just as the traffic light changed from red to green, Tre kept an eye on the three guys as they jumped into a navy blue late model Crown Victoria.

"Check it, that's the boy Tre I was telling y'all about the other day." The driver said while turning on the AC.

"Yo, you sure?" the passenger asked as he wiped the sweat from his forehead.

"Come on dawg, I know who dude is. I don't know how he's getting money, but he's getting some bands!" the driver said.

"Well, start this bitch up then. And follow his ass," the passenger ordered, rubbing his hands together while biting down on his bottom lip. He had been waiting to hit a lick all night.

"Chill, I got this! Just spark that blunt up!" The driver pulled out into the traffic, keeping a safe distance as he tailed his mark.

Still glancing through his rear-view mirror, Tre couldn't help but chuckle, "I know these young mothafuckas don't think shit is that sweet."

At that moment, he pushed a button on his radio to reveal a hidden compartment. After removing and placing the .357 Desert Eagle onto his lap, he picked up his Boost Mobile to alert his homie Nice.

The phone chirped. Nice's voice came through the speaker. "What's the deal big homie?"

"Being followed by some young punks," Tre said.

"What's the situation?"

"Man, I don't know what these fools are up to."

"Where you at?" Nice said, getting angry and restless by the second.

"On Market Street."

"Man, come through the way, I got a treat for them."

"On my way. They're driving in a navy blue old school 4-door."

"Say no more."

Tre and Nice had been close friends since elementary school. From sharing females to selling small time drugs throughout school, there wasn't anything that the two didn't do together. They graduated from Christiana High School but chose the fast life instead of attending college like their smarter friends. Ever since they first met, they vowed to always have each other's backs.

After their brief conversation, Tre turned onto Vandaver Avenue. The trio followed him, making the same turn.

"They don't know what they've gotten themselves into," Tre thought. He hit number three on his CD player and turned the volume up. The lyrics of 50 Cent's song 'Many Men' blasted in the car. A smile sidled across his face as he placed his right hand back onto his automatic weapon. Minutes later and still being shadowed, Tre coasted by Nice's green Dodge Charger. The three young goons followed close behind.

"I think this is where he'll be at," the driver in the old school car announced.

"Well, pull over then," the fat kid from the backseat said, passing a blunt.

"Yeah, let's see what he does," the passenger chimed in.

22nd and Bowers Street was gloomy and unoccupied. Tre parked six cars down from his stalkers, never taking his eyes off of them. He hit the side button of his mobile.

It chirped again. "You see them?" asked Tre.

"Yeah, I got it from here," Nice said, emerging from his parking spot and pulling alongside the trio.

Looking over his left shoulder, the driver in the other car noticed a green Charger with tinted windows just sitting idle. He unrolled his window to get a better view.

"Yo, who the fuck is this?" he shouted at the Charger.

Nice followed suit. He rolled down his passenger side window and brandished a gun. The driver of the Crown Victoria didn't even see it coming. Before he could make sense of what was happening, his brain was splattered over the front window and the dashboard. Leaving no witnesses, Nice unloaded the rest of his clip into the other two passengers. Nosey neighbors swarmed their windows while others took cover. The car's tires screeched as Nice fled the scene with Tre right behind him. Tre chirped the Mobile.

"You straight?" he asked Nice.

"I'm cool, but they're not." Nice replied.

"Listen, tell your little homies to lay low for a few days."

"I got you."

"Holla at me first thing in the a.m. I need to talk with you and the big fella."

"Say no more."

"Good looking on that back there too."

"Any time my nig, any time." Nice turned off on the next street while Tre kept straight.

Tre tossed his mobile and grabbed his other cell phone. With a push of a button, it rang.

"Hello?" a voice came up.

"Whad'up, Sherry?"

"Nothing, just lying in the bed reading this book."

"What book you reading?"

"She Fancy. It's a good read."

"I heard that. What's good, though? You want company?"

"Sure do, daddy. This book already got me hot and horny."

"Well, keep reading. I'll be through in about twenty minutes." He disconnected the call and swerved the car onto the highway, heading towards New Castle.

****

Twenty-five minutes had passed and Sherry was still freshening up when the blaring music invaded her driveway. She knew it was her boo Tre, as she sprayed her Marc Jacobs daisy fragrance in all the right places. Sherry rushed downstairs and opened the front door just as Tre was exiting his car. She bit the bottom part of her lip while shifting her weight from her left leg to the right.

The moonlight danced off Tre's ebony skin. He was tall with an athletic build and dressed in the latest threads; just how she liked her men. Additionally, his wrist was encased by a big-face Cartier watch flooded with diamonds. He grabbed at his crotch while getting an eye full of her curves. Her body was stacked; she could easily be mistaken as a centerfold from a Men's magazine. Her caramel skin complimented her Victoria Secret lingerie, exposing how sexy her curves were.

"Damn, that nigga looks tasty." She used her left hand to play with her nipple while caressing her inner thigh with her right. She didn't care who was watching. Tre brought the freak out of her. No words needed to be spoken. He scooped her up and led her into the house. Their lips touched and tongues locked. He reached between her legs and slid her thong to the side as his middle finger was saturated by her juices, he penetrated her tightness. Their eye contact was strong while his firm touch tightened sending signals to all the right areas.

"Mmmmm, yesssss... right there," she moaned.

Tre didn't want to waste any more time. He removed his finger and smacked Sherry on the ass. "Let's go," he commanded. The two climbed the stairs up to her bedroom.

Once inside, they collapsed on the bed. She held her right ankle up and played with her now swollen clitoris with her free hand. Her breaths were deep.

"It's... getting... real wet... for you, daddy."

The way she called him daddy and the sight of her juice box had him at full attention. Like a kid at Wal-Mart, she observed her toy. Tugging at his shorts, she freed his manhood. Sherry always handled Tre's beefcake with care, elongating him to a good eight inches. She allowed the tip of his penis to rest in the back of her throat, all while licking her tongue up and down his shaft. Tre tore his shirt off, then reached over the back of her pussy and placed two fingers into her wetness. A moan escaped her lips. She took pride in pleasing him. Her aunt always told her, "If you don't do it right, then someone else will." Sherry stretched across the bed and pulled out a gold wrapper. In one motion, within the flash of a second, the condom was out and down his manhood.

Tre was amazed by how quickly she did that. He turned her around and guided himself into the warm wetness of her caramel body. Each stroke was at a forty-five-degree angle, tapping her love button. She smothered the sound of her moan by biting a pillow as her small hands grasped the bedspread for support. After five minutes of intensifying back shots, she climbed on top, saddling him backwards. Holding onto his ankles for support, she performed one of her strengths. Her ass bounced up and down his penis like pogo stick. He palmed both cheeks, driving himself deeper. Without skipping a beat, she spun around, still grinding him into ecstasy. At the point of no return, he released a heavy load off his shoulders, staying with the rhythm. She came too and they both collapsed on the bed, drenched in sweat, exhausted.

Sherry was one of Tre's jump-offs. He would have sex with her whenever he wanted. She was smart, sexy, and had a good head on her shoulders. But to him, she was just another female with a great fuck game. As they lay there, she traced the outlines of his tattoos with her fingers. Without looking up, she said, "Roll som'em up."

The next morning, Tre was awakened by the ringing of his cell phone.

"What's good?" he answered in a raspy tone.

"What's poppin' son? Wake yo ass up!"

"Tommy, whad'up?" Tre said, rising a little. "I'm getting myself together now."

"Nice said you wanted to holler at us. Well, we together now."

"Where y'all at?"

"On our way to Knotty Pine."

"Cool. I'll meet y'all there."

Tommy, short for Thomas, was Tre's friend since his two-year bid on gun charges six years ago. He was from up top, "New York." His dad was knee-deep in the drug game: One day, a state trooper pulled Tommy over while he was driving through Delaware to meet his father. The trooper stopped him for speeding but as he approached the car, the trooper smelled the aroma of weed so he searched the car and found a brick of crack with a gun tucked between the seats. Tommy was arrested so his dad got him the best lawyer money could buy. He escaped a federal indictment and received three years along with another three years of probation.

Tommy met Tre one year into his bid. On a Sunday, during Chapel services, Tre got into a scuffle with four other guys. To this day, Tommy didn't know why he jumped in the fight to

11

help Tre, he just did it. They both were transferred to the Segregated Housing Unit, known as "the hole." They were placed in the same cell and became like brothers. Just like Tommy, Tre was in for drug charges. When the two were released from the hole, they became cellmates to finish out their remaining time. In their conversations, Tre and Tommy found out that their release dates were the same.

On one occasion, the two were outside in the yard playing basketball when two correctional officers approached them and informed Tommy that he needed to come with them. Tre stood there wondering what was going on. That was never a good look; an inmate walking off with the guards. People could get the wrong impression. Tre knew his friend was no snitch, so he wasn't tripping.

Rec yard was over and an hour later, there was still no sign of Tommy. Tre returned to his cell, concerned. When he heard Tommy coming in he just watched him. His eyes widened with shock as Tommy came in, backing up into a corner. Tre approached him knowing something was wrong. "Talk to me, big homie," Tre said.

Tommy was shaking his head from side to side. "It's not true! The mothafuckas don't know what they're talking about."

"What's not true?"

Tommy's big hands covered his head as if he was trying to keep something from getting out.

"Man, fuck that shit. Not my mom dukes and pops."

"Man, whatever it is, we're gonna weather the storm," said Tre

"They gone... a punk ass fire."

Tre didn't know what to say. How could he? He couldn't imagine what Tommy was going through. If it was his mother.

"Homie, I'm sorry to hear that."

"None of it makes sense," Tommy said. "Something tells me that someone killed them. They just trying to use this fire thing as a cover up." He sat down on the metal stool mounted against the wall. His head ached, his thoughts spun, and his eyes watered. "Damn, I wish I was home. None of this would have ever happened. Now I have no home to go to."

"You talking crazy. You'll always have a home as long as I am breathing." Tre meant what he said. Tommy was like family to him now.

"That's love, son. Word. That's real love."

As promised, when they maxed out, Nice was right there to pick them up. He heard a lot about Tommy from the letters Tre sent him. It didn't take long before they were clicking as well. They called themselves 'T.N.T.', short for Tre, Nice, and Tommy. But over the years they spent running the streets, the locals of Wilmington gave them their own name for 'T.N.T.', Them Niggas is Trouble.

Just as Tre ended his call, Sherry awoke. "What, you leaving?"

"Yeah, I have to take care of some business."

"I guess that means I won't be seeing you for a while," she said.

"Come on with the dumb shit, you know what it is."

"I know, daddy, but I be needing my plumbing fixed. You're the only one that got the right tools." She felt played at times; never wanting to accept that she was a mere jump-off for him and nothing more.

He cracked a smile. "Girl, you crazy. Run out to my car and grab the department store bag from the backseat."

"Is there something in there for me?" she exclaimed.

"Hell no, now hurry up and stop playing, girl!" he reproached, smacking her on the ass.

Showered and dressed, he headed out of the front door. It was another hot one and the sun beamed down with force. Tre hopped in his ride, wasting no time turning on the air-conditioner. He grabbed a vanilla Dutch, dumped the guts and filled it with some Kush. He put his Ralph Lauren aviator frames on and started the car. He pushed the button on his CD player. Yound Jeezy featuring Plies 'Lose My Mind' lyrics pumped through the speakers. Tre sped off to meet up with his crew. Pondering what he had to converse about, Tre knew that their lives were about to change for good.

CHAPTER 2: COME UP IS DAYS AWAY

"Damn, this shit is like that." Nice placed the blunt back to his lips and inhaled some more. "Where you get this from?" Nice was loving the way the sweet weed tasted.

"From NY. My peoples got a new batch of that sour diesel," Tommy replied.

"My young boys need this. It'll sell like dope." Nice broke down pounds of exotic weed into twenties. His crew would sell the weed from sunup till sundown. Nice is what you call a cool, laid back type of guy, until you crossed him. He was average height, caramel skin tone with an athletic frame. He was loved by the ladies but feared by his enemies.

"What's the price like?" he asked.

"Dude want like five stacks," said Tommy.

"Five grand, that's not bad. I'm gonna make a lot of money off of this shit."

"Son just got a shipment of that shit in, with mad flavors." He grabbed the blunt and took a few pulls.

"Man, you never spoke of this nigga before." Nice said, his speech slurry. He was zoning out from the weed.

"That's because he came home from the Feds doing a ten year bid. I ran into the dude last week when I went Up Top shopping."

"He ain't going to be on no bullshit, right?"

"Son, this my peoples. He used to put in work for my pops before he got knocked. His word is bond."

"After I knock the rest of this work off, we need to holla at him, for real."

"Say no more, just let a nigga know when you're ready."

In the midst of their conversation, Tre emerged and knocked on the window. It startled the two. Tommy rolled down the window.

"Damn, son, you trying to cause a nigga a heart attack?"

"Y'all going to smoke or we going to eat?" said Tre.

"Nigga, we been waiting on yo ass. Word is bond, I'm hungrier than a mothafucka."

Tre reached his arm in the window, giving them both some hand daps. "Well, I'm here now. Let's eat and handle this B.I."

"We right behind you, kid," said Tommy, taking a few more pulls before putting out the rest of the blunt.

Tre shook his head and turned around. He entered Knotty Pine; He loved this place. He had been eating there ever since he was a kid. Moms, the owner, made the best breakfast and fish sandwiches in Wilmington. He seated himself in the last booth by the kitchen.

Moms came out of the kitchen door and spotted him. "Tre."

"Hey, Moms," he rose and gave her a kiss on the cheek.

"You want your usual?" she asked.

"Yes, please, but make that three orders. Nice and Tommy is out front," he told her as he sat back down.

"I'll make that four orders then. You and I both know that Tommy can eat," she chuckled before disappearing in the back. Tre laughed. While waiting, he saw a local newspaper nearby and started reading it.

Minutes later, Tommy rambled through the front door. At 6' 6", three hundred pounds, you couldn't even tell that Nice was behind him. He was dark skinned with a smooth head. Many mistook him as a professional football player. The two joined the table just as Tre threw the newspaper down. It read under the headline, 'Gun shots rang out late last night on the northeast of Wilmington, leaving three young males dead. The shootings are believed to be drug-related. So far, there have been no leads on the investigation. Detective Smith is asking anyone with any information to come forward and contact him at the city of Wilmington Police Department.'

"Y'all just call me the professional," gloated Nice as he took a seat.

"Son, if I was there, it would've read, 'Three Young Males Choked to Death,' ya heard?"

Nice smirked. "You hear this nigga? Just 'cause yo big ass eats whole chicken and lifts dumpsters for a living. Now you want to choke a nigga? Keep it up and a mothafucka gonna pop yo big ass too."

"I keep my fifty," retorted Tommy, referring to his 50 caliber handgun.

Tre interjected. "Man, that shit is done and over with. Let's get down to business. Peep game, I know y'all tired of penny pinching, right? Nice, you flipping what, two to three pounds a month?"

"Yeah."

He looked at Tommy. "We're both keeping our heads above water with this coke shit. It's time to step our game up, and I mean all the way up."

"I feel you, but prices are mad crazy. My peoples up top won't budge on them numbers unless we step up our re-up."

"Exactly! That's where my peoples Magic's plan comes into play."

"What's he talking about?" Nice was eager to know.

"Check it, he's been scoping this heavy hitter's every move. He said dude's holding heavy paper."

Tommy leaned forward. "Holding how much?"

"Like a half a mill in cash, and about fifteen joints of that down south finest."

Tommy's adrenaline began pumping, "Now we're talking." He was already counting his share of the money.

"They better get some body bags ready," said Nice. He didn't know who they were, but they were about to be added to his body count. "Son, when this shit supposed to pop off?"

"This weekend, so handle everything that needs to be handled 'cause we're flying out on Friday morning," said Tre.

"Flying! Now... you know I hate flying," said Tommy. Just the thought of it was enough to make him sick. "Plus what are we gonna do about our fire power? Can't take that on no plane, ya heard?"

"We won't be needing to, Magic gonna handle all of that on his end. We just need to get down there."

"I'm with it," Nice agreed.

"Fuck it, I'm in." Though Tommy didn't want to get on a plane, for the love of money, he'd fly to the other side of the world and back any day.

Moms came out and placed their plates of steak, egg and cheese along with side bowls of buttered grits. She placed each platter in front of them as they all rubbed their hands.

"Y'all boys ready to eat?"

"Yes," came the united response.

Moms went back and brought beverages. As she left, the three ate in silence, each lost in his thoughts.

Tre left Knotty Pine and headed back home in his car, listening to Power 99 FM. He hadn't been home since yesterday and knowing his dog, 'Psycho,' his apartment was going to be a mess. He was in deep thought when the host on the radio caught his attention.

"It's going down tonight! Dress to impress. Our Philly Queen 'Evey Eve' is throwing a party at Taj Mahal in Atlantic City, New Jersey! The after party will be held at the 40/40 Club. Come out and party with us! Tickets will be sold at the door."

I can't miss it Tre thought to himself. Turning the volume down, he alerted Nice on his boost mobile.

"What's good?" said Nice.

"You still with Tommy?"

"Yeah, I'm about to drop his big ass off to his truck now."

"Y'all trying to step out tonight? They doing it real big up A.C."

"We're with it."

"Throw that shit on."

"We always do," Nice let it be known.

"I'm about to call my travel agent to book us a room at the Taj Mahal.

"Say no more, what time we out?"

"Eight o' clock."

Minutes later, Tre hung up the call from his travel agent. She booked them a party room that connected to a Grand View Suite, plus three tickets to attend the party.

Tre smiled as he grabbed the half-blunt from the ashtray. He lit it while taking in deep pulls. Just in case shit went wrong with Magic, he would make sure they did it up tonight. Tre hit number one on his CD player, then turned up the volume. Jay Z now pumped loud through his speakers.

CHAPTER 3: SOMETIMES YOU GOT TO GET AWAY

Casina and her girlfriend Lolita had just flown in from Miami. Casina, needing a getaway from her over-protective twin brothers, had been itching for a vacation. Her brothers had only agreed to it because it would give them time to handle their out-of-town business for a couple of days. Thanks to her BFF Lolita, they had just landed at Philadelphia International Airport. The two now awaited Lolita's friends from college, Terry and Meshia, who were from Newcastle, Delaware.

Life for Casina wasn't always this strict. Her African American father, Ricky Jones Sr., aka 'RJ', was a notorious kingpin out of Miami, Florida. He had it all and everything was under his control, from the streets to the night clubs. RJ took good care of his wife Vanessa, a Brazilian beauty; his twin boys, Ricky Jr. and Rayman; and of course his baby girl, Casina. Casina was allowed to do as she pleased but her brothers, jealous, would always try to get her in trouble with their father. It didn't matter what she was doing, her brothers would always find a way to tell their father something. It wasn't like they didn't like her or wanted to get her in some serious trouble. They just knew the streets all too well and wanted Casina to avoid the drama. By far, RJ never wanted his daughter in the street either, but he also didn't want to shelter her. He knew she was safe. After all, he ran Miami and people knew not to fuck with his family, especially his little princess.

Life couldn't be better for Casina until one dreadful day she came home early from college. The road that lead towards her parent's mansion was flooded with marked and unmarked police vehicles. Seeing these vehicles in her neighborhood was unprecedented. You'd only see the police around these parts if the area needed to be evacuated due to bad weather. Reaching the front gates of her parent's home, Casina set her eyes on the gossiping neighbors, news reporters, and armed policemen. The insignia across their chest didn't just represent local police, but FBI, AFT, and DEA agents.

To her surprise, her father was out on the balcony armed with an AK-47. She heard him yelling at the top of his lungs, "Y'all mothafuckas are fucking with the wrong one! I run this shit right here!" At that moment, Casina's father noticed her and their eyes met. Even from the distance, she could read her father's lips. His last words, "I love you, baby girl."

Tears started flowing down Casina's cheeks as her father squeezed the trigger. Bullets pierced through the Federal agent's body armors, knocking them down one by one. That only lasted a few seconds before a sniper shot RJ between his eyes. Casina's heart stopped as she watched her father's lifeless body lean over the rail and fall through the gazebo. Agents raided the mansion and brought out Ricky Jr., Rayman, and Vanessa, all in handcuffs. It was Casina's worst day of her life.

Thanks to their mother, Ricky and Rayman were both released six months later; she had taken all the charges. Vanessa was later found guilty and sentenced to life in a federal prison. Seven months into her bid, she'd committed suicide. With the death of both parents, Ricky and Rayman took over the family business, causing mayhem throughout the streets of Miami and the surrounding areas. That's when Casina's life became a living hell. Her brothers gave her everything she desired, but love was absent from her life. Making matters worse, every time she was involved in a real relationship, her brothers would always chase the guy away. A while back, Casina was dating a guy from college when he received a visit from her brothers. He never showed his face around campus again. She tried to call but his number would go straight to voice mail. Lord only knew what they said or did to him.

Still waiting for Terry and Meshia to arrive, Casina and Lolita stood in front of Terminal F with their Louis Vuitton luggage, looking flawless. Lolita was no slouch, styling in her yellow and gold maxi dress. She was a short Spanish beauty, with short, thick red hair and a body that men dreamed of. To approach her, you needed money coming out of your pockets. But still, all in all, she was no match for Casina.

At five-eight, one hundred and fifty pounds, Casina's frame had an exotic look. Her skin had a smooth caramel complexion. She had a black-and-white Prada tank top on. Underneath, her 34c-sized breasts contradicted gravity without needing a bra.

Running track daily at her college campus had given her an alluring body, flat abs, and stunning legs. You couldn't forget the Brazilian ass her mother had blessed her with. It rested under her black cut-off Prada shorts. Her long black, feather-like hair hung midway down the middle of her back with mysterious hazel eyes and sexy lips complimenting her attractive face.

"Ah, ya two fine beauties need a ride?" an African taxi driver cruised by and asked.

"No, we're waiting for our friend. Thanks anyway," Lolita replied. Just then, Terry came into view, driving a cherry red BMW 535 sedan. It had pearl white interior leather with the red trim and an exotic wood grain steering wheel. Bopping to Remy Ma's song, ' I look good to be wearing this, I got a reason, I'm conceited,' Terry hopped out at the sight of Lolita screaming,

"Whass'up, gurl!"

"Nothing gurl, look at you. I'm loving the car," Lolita replied, giving her a girly hug.

"Yeah, my baby daddy takes care of me," said Terry with pride in her voice.

"Where's Meshia at? I thought she was coming too."

"Gurl, the shop was jam-packed. She still had one more head to do."

"Oh, I'm tripping, Terry. This is my girl, Casina, I was telling you about," Lolita said, introducing Casina to her.

"Hey, gurl, any friend of Lolita's is a friend of mine."

"Nice to meet you. I've heard so much about you," smiled Casina.

"I hope good things," replied Terry, checking out their luggage.

"Gurl, stop it," Lolita said.

"I'm loving the luggage. Put it in the trunk and let's go. We have a big night ahead of us. We're going to Eve's party tonight, everybody that is a somebody is going to be there." Terry informed them both.

"Yes, 'cause I'm in need of a good time," Casina thought to herself.

"I hope Meisha's not tired, 'cause a bitch needs her hair touched-up," said Lolita.

"You think she would do something with mine too?" Casina asked.

"Hell yeah, that bitch loves money," replied Terry, while pulling off.

CHAPTER 4: WE BALLIN' LIKE WE LIVE IN THE TAJ MAHAL

Back at his apartment, Tre scurried around as if his head was chopped off, cleaning up after his dog, Psycho. Psycho was a blue nosed pit-bull, short and stocky with a big-ass head. Tre got him from a Kennel website off of the Internet for $1,400 dollars. After cleaning up the mess Psycho made, Tre scanned his apartment. For him to be a bachelor, his spot wasn't that bad. But Tre was a man of ambition, he wanted more and better. Ten years ago, he would never have imagined his life to turn out like this. He always had dreams of being successful and owning his own businesses one day. He even had thoughts about going to college to get a degree in business and management. But when the mean streets got a hold of him, all that was positive went straight out of the window. It didn't help that he didn't have a father figure in his life at all. Tre remembered like it was yesterday when his mother had always said, "I'm your mother and father." Breaking his train of thoughts, Tre went to his safe in the closet. He pushed a few buttons on the keypad and it opened. There, in front of him, was twenty-five thousand dollars in cash. He grabbed just five thousand for tonight's events. His mind wandered off to the conversation between him and his cousin Magic.

Damn, I hope this shit pops off. It's some moves I'm trying to make, he thought to himself.

Later that night...

Casina, Lolita, Terry, and Meshia were about to head out to the Casbar. It was a Tuesday night and they were ready to go downstairs and get their groove on. Lolita was styling in a red Versace dress that fit her body just right, with a pair of matching red pumps. "A devil in disguise," she admired herself as she sauntered past a full-length mirror. Terry had on a black-and-gold Gucci halter top dress that belayed right under her ass, so that if she was to bend over, everybody at the club would know her business.

Terry yelled to her girlfriends, "Damn! I'm fine!"

Meshia yelled back, "Whatever!" Meshia was wearing a Prada one-piece with her back out to show off her Leo tattoo. The three of them waited in the living room of their Hotel Suite, admiring each other's outfits when Lolita yelled, "Come on, Casina, why does it always take you the longest to get dressed?"

"Shut up, I'm coming now," Casina replied. She strolled into the room and the three looked in stupefied silence. Casina wore a smile as if it was her wedding day. She was wearing an exclusive blue Louis Vuitton shirt dress that showed off her hourglass curves and stopped beneath her ass. She wore a necklace that looked like she paid a pretty penny for it. Her shoes were the same blue as her dress with silver diamonds around the trim. Thanks to Meshia, her hair had reddish color highlights. She had long layers and had it feather-curled all over. Casina was super sexy and she knew it. "Are y'all ready to go or what, 'cause a bitch is ready to show her ass tonight," she said, rubbing her hands down her curves.

*****

Now back upstairs in his suite, Tre tried his luck and came up. He turned his $5,000 into $12,000 by playing Spanish 21. Standing in front of a full-length mirror, he was checking out his black tightly fitted Tom Ford t-shirt and his dark blue distressed Tom Ford jeans. He also rocked a pair of black Cole Haan shoes to set off his attire. The waves in his hair looked like they came straight of off the Pacific Ocean. "I need to be posing in one of those GQ magazines," he bragged to himself.

"Son, you need to come on so we can be out," Tommy said, walking up to him. He was wearing a pair of Tru Religion jeans and a black short sleeve button-up shirt, with black Gucci loafers and a matching belt.

"I'm ready, let's roll," Tre replied. The two walked into the party room to get Nice. Nice was listening to music, wearing a black linen outfit with a pair of Prada shoes. The three of them exited the suite heading downstairs to get the party popping.

The Club...

When they arrived, the club was packed, and the line was long as hell.

"I'm too cute to be standing in some damn line just to get up in some damn club," protested Terry, looking at the many partiers that stood before her.

"Yeah, me too," added Meshia, while checking out the many sharp fellas that were in line. As she stood next to her friends, Casina took notice of a gentleman gazing at her. She acted as if she didn't even notice him. They finally got into the club where R. Kelly's 'I'm a flirt' was loudly playing. Lolita went right for the dance floor with Terry tailing behind her. Casina and Meshia headed straight towards the bar for some drinks. As soon as Casina found a stool to sit down on, someone tapped Casina on her shoulder. She turned around to see the same gentleman from earlier, now standing behind her.

"Hello, beautiful," he said, as he eyed her from head to toe.

Casina looked and responded, "Hello."

"What's your name, if you don't mind me asking?"

"Casina. And yours?"

"I'm Craig, nice to meet you."

"Nice to meet you also," she replied.

He asked her if he could get her and her friend a drink while pulling out a wad of money. Casina turned away nonchalantly, rolled her eyes and said, "No, thanks."

"That's ok. Do you have a number so I can get in touch with you?"

"I don't give out my number to people in the club, sweetie," she informed him.

"Is there any way we can meet up outside the club, then?"

"Maybe we will meet up one day outside the club," she replied, not really feeling this guy. Craig walked away, disappointed.

Meshia looked at her like she was crazy. "What's wrong, gurl? He was fine as shit. Did you see all that money, gurl?"

"Money is not everything."

"You right, but if he's willing to throw it away, then why not catch it?" remarked Meshia.

"Whatever girl, you crazy and besides I have my eyes on something better and he's standing right over there." Casina had eyed the sexiest man she'd ever seen. Looking in that direction, Meshia noticed who she was looking at.

"Ohhh, shit. Gurl, that's Tre."

"You know him?" Casina inquired.

"Yeah, he's from up my way. That man is fine as shit. He must have noticed you noticing him 'cause he's looking over here," said Meshia.

Just then, Lolita and Terry came over from the dance floor and yelled, "What y'all going to do? Hold up the bar all night?" Before they could answer, 'UNK' Walk it Out came on and they all were back on the dance floor, except for Casina, whose eyes were glued on Tre. She was loving his whole appearance as the spot lights shined off his dark complexion. Casina didn't know what it was about him but it was drawing her to him.

CHAPTER 5: LOVE AT FIRST SIGHT

In the middle of the dance floor, Tre was staring at the beauty seated at the bar. He leaned over to Tommy to speak "I'll be back, I'm heading over to the bar to get some more Rose'."

Tommy, not really paying him any mind, nodded his head while still grinding up on a big booty female he had just met. Tre maneuvered through the crowd with swagger. Every female that he passed was ogling him from head to toe. Not once did he stop to entertain the attention; his thoughts and eyes were occupied by her beauty.

Reaching the bar area, Tre yelled over the loud music to the bartender, "Excuse me, can I get another bottle of Rosé?" Casina looked to her left and smiled. Tre took notice and after paying the tab, slid in her direction.

"You know, it's rude to stare," he joked.

"I wasn't staring at you," said Casina, feeling embarrassed.

"I'm just playing. My name is Tre. Yours?"

"Casina." The two locked eyes like pit bulls in heat. Tre admired her flowing hair and the way she looked in her Louis Vuitton dress.

Damn, she looks good as shit. I got to get me some of that, he thought to himself, "So, Casina, that's a beautiful name. Where you from?"

"Miami."

"Miami huh? What brings you up this way?"

"Let's just say I was in need of a vacation," she replied.

"You know, we got a lot in common already."

"Oh, do we?"

"Yes, we're both very interested in getting to know each other too," he teased.

The two were deep into their conversation when T-Pain's song 'Let me buy you a drink' came on. Tre gave her the look that said, "Let's dance," and the two headed straight towards the dance floor.

Four songs later, things started to get hot and heavy. By this time, it was 1:30 a.m. and Casina was feeling tipsy from the Rosé Tre had given her. From the bulge in Tre's jeans, she knew it was time to find her friends before she got herself in trouble.

On their way back to the bar, Tre informed her about his party room. Casina told him that she had to find her friends and would discuss it with them. He gave her his suite and cell phone number before walking off.

Minutes later, Casina found her friends looking just as tipsy. She informed them about Tre and his party room. They had other plans; they were on their way to the Jay Z's 40/40 club. Little did they know Casina had plans of her own. Suite 1141 was all she was thinking about as she headed towards the exit.

*****

Casina reached Suite 1141 and heard soft music being played from the other side. She knocked twice and felt awkward and out of place. Just as she changed her mind and turned back from the door to leave, Tre opened it. "You weren't about to leave so quick now, were you?"

"I didn't know if I was at the right suite or now," she lied, blushing.

"So you decided to come alone, I see?"

"Yeah, my friends ditched me for the 40/40."

"Don't feel bad. Mine's did too," Tre replied, leading Casina in. Once inside, Casina was amazed. *This is nothing like our suite* she thought to herself. Tre escorted her to the living room. "Would you like some Rosé?" he asked, while holding up the cold bottle.

"Yes, please."

After pouring two glasses of Rosé, Tre sat down beside her. With the music low, they engaged in a deep conversation while sipping from their wine glasses. All of a sudden, 112 started playing through the speakers.

"Here we are alone, you and me, privacy... that's my song!" Casina proclaimed, moving to the beat.

"Well, if that's the case, can I have this dance?" he asked, turning the volume up a little bit. The two of them danced away like wedding couples in the middle of the floor. Their bodies were so close that Tre's thigh was rubbing the inside of her leg, making her love canal soaking wet. She could feel the warmth and the wetness starting to run down her inner leg. Feeling the vibe she was giving, Tre started kissing her neck while pulling her in closer. His lips felt like magic to her and she was loving every bit of it. Her moans grew louder and she wrapped her arms around his neck. Lifting her up, Tre led her into the Master

Suite room, grabbing some ice from the bucket along the way. As he crunched the ice, he started kissing and sucking all over her.

Feeling good, but awkward at the same time, Casina snapped back to reality and spoke, "I can't do this, I'm sorry if I led you on."

Tre sensed how uncomfortable she was and replied, "It's ok, sweetie, we can just finish enjoying each other's company." With that said, within an hour, they were both cuddled up with each other, fast asleep.

The next morning, Tre was awoken by his homies. "Son, get yo ass up!" Tommy yelled, throwing a pillow at him. Tre, adjusting his eyes to the light, looked around for Casina.

"Where is she, where's Casina?"

"Casina? Who the fuck is Casina?" asked Nice, confused.

"Nothing, never mind," replied Tre as he got up. *Damn, she must have left. I didn't get a chance to get her number* he thought to himself.

"Man, fuck that Casina chick. We need to go downstairs to the casino and try to win some chips, you dig?" Nice stated as he fired up a blunt.

"Son, I'm with you on that one but a nigga got to eat first. I'm hungry as shit," said Tommy. He pushed the room service button on the phone.

"Nigga, yo ass always hungry!" Nice laughed as he inhaled deep pulls.

"Whatever, nigga. Pass that blunt, Smokey," replied Tommy.

Still trying to get himself together, Tre found himself still stuck on Casina. *Damn, I hope she calls a brother* he thought to himself.

CHAPTER 6: STICK 'EM UP, STICK 'EM UP

Days rolled by and Casina was still vividly on Tre's mind, but yet he couldn't understand why she hadn't called him yet. Never, out of all of his years of dating has a female had his mind so gone. Tommy sensed something was on Tre's mind and decided to confront him.

"Son, I know you're not thinking about shawty again. She must've been the bomb, 'cause she got you open."

"It's not that. It's just something about her. Something about that night was magic," Tre said, staring off into space.

"Speaking of magic, where's yo peoples at anyway? We've been waiting for a nice minute now," Nice added, checking out the scenery.

They had recently arrived in Atlanta, Georgia. The temperature was up and the gorgeous females were flocking. They all awaited in the Avis parking lot. There was still no sight of Magic.

"Man, let's ride around and check out a few spots. You see all these bitches out here?" Nice said, looking around.

"Stay focused. He said he'll be here," Tre replied.

Ten minutes later, Tre's phone went off. Seeing that it was Magic, he answered, "Where you at?" Tre asked feeling kind of frustrated.

"Calm down, baby boy. I'm behind you," Magic said.

Tre looked through his rearview mirror and spotted a black Chevy. "That's you in the black Chevy?"

"Yup. Now follow me up out of this bitch, cuz," he replied, backing out and pulling off.

Forty minutes later, now at Magic's place, the four of them went over the master plan detail by detail, making sure every angle was covered. There was a light tapping sound at the front door. Magic removed his pistol from his waistband, turning it sideways he trained it on the door. "Who the fuck is it?"

"It's me, sweetie," a female voice replied from the other side of the door. Magic unlocked the door and opened it. A dark and lovely beauty came strutting in, curvaceous to death. All eyes were glued on her as she headed towards Magic".

"Gentlemen, this here is the key to our fortune. I would like y'all to meet Linda." Magic introduced her to others while wrapping his arm around her lower back area.

She looked up at him," The van is parked outside, baby."

"That's my bonnie," Magic praised Linda. He then turned and grabbed a black duffle bag. Unzipping it, he showed them the guns they had requested while completing the explanation of his blueprint.

Tre felt bad vibes about Linda, but it was too late now, because tonight it was definitely going down.

*****

It was a beautiful night and the parking lot of Magic City was packed to capacity. It was one of Atlanta's hottest strip clubs. It looked like a set from a rap video with enough diamonds and chrome rims to light up the Falcon's Stadium. Inside was an off-the-wall and plush atmosphere, with enough booty clapping and shaking to turn a gay man straight. If you were looking for a great time and a high-powered night, the legendary Magic City was the place to be. Too bad they wouldn't be able to enjoy what Magic City had to offer.

"Yo, there he go. Oh yea, this shit should be easy. Wait, wait, let's go," Nice said. Him, Tre, and Tommy were leaving Magic City strip club trailing a nice distance behind Fat Cat. Fat Cat was driving in a money-green GL550 Benz with rims. He was the big-time drug dealer Magic had informed them about. Fat Cat got his name cause of his bank roll. Locals always told him, "You're eating like a fat cat." The nickname stuck with him ever since.

From the way Nice said he was throwing money up in the strip joint, they knew it was going to be a big pay day.

Let's just hope Linda comes through on her end, Tre thought while making a left hand turn. Linda worked for Fat Cat, but was also fucking Magic on the side. Magic convinced her to help him get the drop on Fat Cat. Like a loyal sex slave, she was, she came through. Once a month, Fat Cat, two of his most trustworthy soldiers, and Linda counted up his money for his out-of-town connect at the stash house. Tonight was that night, with a man on the inside...woman, that is. Nothing could go wrong.

Driving to a secluded area, they watched as Fat Cat and his two goons exited the Benz. They hesitated at first while checking out their surroundings before entering the house. Like clockwork, ten minutes later, Linda pulled up. Exiting her ride, she winked over at the tan van with tinted windows. Inside, waiting patiently was Fat Cat's worst nightmare.

Two hours had passed and the three of them were still waiting.

"Showtime!" Tre announced. Linda was standing in the window giving them their cue. As they checked their guns, they made sure each of them were ready. Pulling down their fitted caps, and checking the scenery, they exited the van while walking expeditiously to their destination. Each of them was dressed in all black and carried a duffel bag. With gloves on their hands and their hands tightly gripping their weapons, Tre knocked on the door. "Knock! Knock! Knock!"

Inside, Linda reacted. "I'll get it." She moved fast towards the door.

Sensing something was wrong, Fat Cat yelled. "Bitch! Don't you open that -"

Before he could even finish his sentence, the door was slung open and the three armed men stood before them. Feeling like his world had just been snatched from him, Fat Cat's mind went blank. Tre snatched Linda up in his arms with his gun trained on her head.

Everybody, get the fuck down on the ground with your hands out in front of you or the bitch will get it!" Tre barked. "

Linda screamed, "Oh my God, please don't kill me!" She was putting on a show and if this was a film, she would have been nominated for the best female actress.

The three complied and got face-down on the ground. Fat Cat tried to be sneaky and started reaching for his gun, but Nice was all over him. "Try to play superman, my nig, and my bullet will be your kryptonite." Nice assured him while disarming the three.

"Who are y'all and what do you want?" Fat Cat asked in fear. He really didn't want the intruders to answer that last question, 'cause in the back of his mind, he knew why they were here. He just was trying to figure out who betrayed him.

"Nigga, shut the fuck up! You know what it is. Where's the money at?" Tre snarled. His adrenaline was now pumping at rapid speed. Turning back wasn't an option at this point.

"All I got is a little over ten thousand. Take it," Fat Cat offered. He scanned the faces of his two goons and Linda's. *Which one of you fuckers was it,* he thought to himself.

"That nigga lying, the safe is in the back," Linda blurted out. She wasn't trying to waste any more time. Fat Cat looked at her wide-eyed, surprised, "You stupid bitch! I'll kill you!" he snarled.

"My dude, shut yo bitch ass up!" Tommy said. Gripping the back of Fat Cat's neck, Tommy lifted him nearly a foot off the ground, leading him towards the back of the house. Tre followed behind him while Nice stayed in the front room with Linda and the two soldiers.

In the back room, Tre wasted no time. "Open the fucking safe!"

"Do you know who I am?" Fat Cat warned. He really wasn't the gangster type but his life was on the line.

"Wrong answer!" Tre replied, hitting him on the back of his head with the .357 Desert Eagle.

"Fuck, man! Why you do that? I told you, I can't open that safe. If I do, I'm a dead man," Fat Cat pleaded, while holding the back of his head. Blood oozed through his fingers.

"Nigga, you think it's a game! You think I'm playing? Tommy, do what you do." Tre ordered.

That's all Tommy wanted to hear. "Son, we told you to open the fucking safe, right?" Tommy warned, while snatching off his chain. With force, he took hold of Fat Cat's throat, suddenly cutting off his windpipe. Fighting for breath, the only possible thing he could do was look into Tommy's fearless eyes. That alone scared the shit out of him. But still, he knew by opening that safe, he would be good as dead. Clenching his throat even tighter, Tommy grabbed one of his fingers and broke it like a stick. Still staring him in his eyes, Fat Cat wanted to yell but couldn't. He tried to put up a struggle with him, but that was no match for Tommy's strength. Still in all, that didn't stop the tears from cascading down his face.

"Man up, nigga. You ready to talk now?" Tre asked as he paced back and forth. Not able to talk, Fat Cat nodded his head up and down. Tommy released his death grip. Fat Cat didn't hesitate to give up the codes to the safe.

After opening the safe, Tre's eyes dropped. Never in his life had he seen so many dead presidents. "Jackpot! Nigga, we rich. You hear me? We fucking rich!" Tre blurted out in happiness.

Fat Cat sat defeated, watching Tre and Tommy fill up the duffle bags with his connect money. He knew he was a dead man one way or another. After the last bag was filled, Tre turned and gave Tommy a nod while walking towards the front room.

"My dude, think of a happy thought," was all Tommy said before shoving his .50 caliber gun down Fat Cat's throat and squeezing the trigger.

Tre entered into the front room to see Nice already handling business. Nice had a trash bag in one of his hands with both soldiers down on their knees, side by side. With his .40 caliber trained at the temple of one, pulling the trigger once was all it took.

"Now that's what I call killing two birds with one bullet," Nice stated with a smirk on his face.

They all fled the house and jumped into the van. "What a piece of cake," Tre thought while fleeing the scene with Linda tailing behind them. Too bad they didn't notice one of Fat Cat's workers slouched down in the seat of his car. Too scared to react to the situation, he was only thinking of one person and one person only.

Linda....

CHAPTER 7: YOU SNOOZE, YOU LOSE

Coming out of a restaurant located in downtown Atlanta on Peachtree, Rayman and Ricky were both stuffed from some good old southern cooking.

"Damn, bro, you still on the phone?" Rayman asked, checking his stocks off of his BlackBerry.

"This mothafucka is playing games! I done called this fuck boy three times, and he still not answering!" Ricky barked, pushing the end button on his cell.

"Calm down bro, maybe he's still counting the money," suggested Rayman, noticing that his stocks were doing well.

"Fuck that, this lame-ass nigga still should have answered the damn phone. Come on so that we can ride by the stash house," replied Ricky, jumping in the rental truck.

*****

Back at Magic's place, Tre watched in awe as they counted up the money. "How much is it?" he asked, stopping in front of the table.

"Word the mother, I know I'm not tripping. It's like one point eight here," Tommy informed him in shock, not believing it himself.

"One-point-eight million! Are you sure?" Tre asked in disbelief.

"Man, we counted this three times already," Nice assured him, while pointing at the piles of money in front of them.

"And how much work did you say you got from the front room, Nice?" Tre asked.

"Twenty bricks," Nice affirmed. They all stared at the coke and the money for a brief moment until Tre broke the silence between them.

"Divide that shit up, we got things to do."

Tre's mind was going a hundred miles per hour. When it was all said and done, Magic and Linda got $450,000 and ten bricks. Tre, Tommy, and Nice on the other hand got $450,000 a piece, plus ten bricks of coke to break down between them.

"Cuz, you sure you don't want more of the cut?" Tre asked.

"This all we need, trust me cuz, we straight," Magic assured him.

"Thanks, big cuz. You just don't know, we needed this," replied Tre.

"No, thank you," said Magic, giving them all daps. "Drive safe, and hit me when y'all touch down." Magic added before walking them out.

The drive back was going to be a living hell; driving up Interstate 95 North with a little over a million dollars in cash and ten bricks of that down south finest would have any hustler shitting bricks. Tommy as well as Nice were lost deep in their own thoughts, but Tre's mind started wondering back to Casina.

*****

Pulling to the stash house, Ricky and Rayman noticed Fat Cat's Benz parked out front. Ricky grew angry. "This nigga was here the whole time! And still hasn't hit me back. He got some explaining to do. And look, bro, he got his Benz parked out front. Is he stupid or what? That's some straight up hot shit!" he barked.

Rayman looked over at his brother and shook his head. As they exited the vehicle, they stormed right up to the door. "BOOM! BOOM! BOOM!" No one answered and that pissed Ricky off even more.

"Something feels wrong," Rayman whispered, as he reached for his weapon. Going with their conscience, they both observed their surroundings. Ricky reached for the door knob. It was unlocked. They both entered the house with their guns aimed high.

"What the fuck is this?" they both said in unison at the sight of the two bodies in front of them. Rayman scanned the room for movement while Ricky moved towards the back room, Rayman on his heels. In the back room, Ricky spotted Fat Cat slumped on his head with the back of his neck blown out. Rayman looked to the left and noticed the empty safe wide open.

"It's gone!" he snapped with attitude.

"Fuck! Somebody's going to die," Ricky muttered through clenched teeth, kicking the dead body. He couldn't believe his eyes. Who had the balls to pull off something like this?

The noise behind them made them both turn around simultaneously with their guns leveled to kill.

"Please don't shoot!" Fat Cat's worker yelled with his hands out in front of him.

"Who the fuck is you?" Ricky demanded. He was ready to blow his brains away if he heard the wrong thing.

"I-I-I work for Fat Cat," the young worker stuttered nervously. The sight of Fat Cat's lifeless body made him sick to the stomach.

"What the fuck happened here?" Rayman wanted to know, his gun still aimed at the worker's head.

"Li-Linda did this," he managed to blurt out.

"Wait a minute. You mean to tell me that some bitch came up in here, killed three niggas and got away with our money?" Ricky snarled, ready to shoot the kid's face off for lying to him.

"No, she set him up. Three niggas that I never seen before was in on it," the worker added.

"And you know where this bitch rests at?" Rayman asked.

"No, but I can find out."

"You do that," Ricky said, passing him a number to contact them.

"Hold up, let me see your ID," Rayman demanded. Giving up his ID, Fat Cat's worker was confused. "This is insurance, 'cause if you don't find this bitch, then we will find you. And kill everyone that's close to you," Rayman assured him. Before leaving, they told the worker to torch the place.

Meanwhile, out front, Trap watched like a hawk as the two dreadlock men pulled off. "Damn, they look alike," he thought as he checked his guns. Looking over at his little homie, who was checking his guns as well, he said, "You ready to do this, shawty?" Before his little homie could respond, the stash house went up in flames.

"What the fuck? What type of shit is this? Pull up out of this bitch. Damn Slow Juice is going to be pissed," Trap cursed to his little homie.

Making a clean getaway through the back door, Fat Cat's worker was on his mission to find Linda.

CHAPTER 8: HOME SWEET HOME

The sun became visible as they headed along I-95. Like a baby, Tommy was passed out in the back seat. Tre and Nice spotted the Twelfth Street's half-mile sign.

"About time, I'm in need of a blunt bad as shit," Nice let it be known as he adjusted himself in his seat.

"Me and you both. This drive was stressful as shit. I swear, every car looked like po-po," Tre added, taking the Twelfth Street exit. A few minutes later, they were pulling up on 22nd & Bowers Street. Tre parked.

"Wake yo big ass up!" Nice shouted.

"Damn son, you don't have to be all loud and shit. I can hear you," Tommy grunted.

"Alright now, y'all get your shit together. I'm going to put this shit up before heading to the airport to get my car. I'll get up with y'all later tonight so that we can split this work up. Oh yeah, before I forget, WE RICH BITCH!" Tre yelled with excitement. Tommy and Nice both agreed before exiting the rental, laughing.

Tre sat in silence for a minute as he replayed the events that had just taken place. With his newly found fortune, he would finally be able to accomplish some of the things he wanted so badly to get done. Without a doubt, he knew his life was about to change for the better. Breaking his train of thoughts, his cell phone went off. Picking it up, he shook his head at the caller ID on his screen.

"What's good?" he answered.

"Hey, daddy. You don't love me no more?" came the reply.

"Damn, Sherry, how did you know I was even back in town yet?"

"Boy, please. You know my dick detector is on point," she stated, popping her gum over the phone.

"You funny, what's good though?"

"I was wondering if I could see you tonight," she asked, hoping his answer would be a yes.

"I don't know. I just got back in town, so I'm not going to make any promises. I have a few things to handle tonight."

"I thought I could be one of those things you would be handling," she whined, feeling disappointed.

"Look, Sherry, just let me handle this B.I., and I'll call you later."

"OK, daddy," she replied before hanging up her phone.

******

Later that evening, Tre regained consciousness from a long nap. He stretched and reached for his cell phone. Checking the screen of his Iphone, he saw three missed calls. One from Tommy, one from Nice, and the other from C-low. The missed calls from Tommy and Nice could wait; it was C-low who he needed to talk to as soon as possible. Pushing the talk button, the phone started to ring.

C-low was in his early twenties, half black and half Puerto Rican. He resided on the west side of Wilmington, Delaware. West side was the biggest sector of Wilmington. Tre met C-low from his big performance at a summer league basketball game a few years back. He dropped forty points against the east side team, helping Tre win a $1,000 bet he had against some hustler from the east side area. After the game, Tre introduced himself to C-low and hit him off with two hundred dollars. C-low didn't know why he was getting the money in the first place but he didn't complain either. Ever since then, they quickly built a close relationship. Once Tre really started kicking it with him, he began hitting him off with some work from time to time. C-low was very smart; it was like hustling was his second nature. In no time, he and his crew had a block on smash. With Tre's recent come-up, he knew he could easily help C-low take over a nice part of the west side area.

After a brief conversation with C-low, that basically sealed the deal. Tre was going to give him four bricks on consignment, at $24,000 a brick. He knew the work was good, but he didn't know how good. So with that said, Tre was going to give him a month to pay him back.

Picking up his cell phone, Tre dialed Tommy and Nice, telling them both to meet him at Battlefield Park located on the northeastern part of Wilmington. After showering and throwing some clothes on, he then grabbed the bricks; dividing four into one bag. He then divided three in two separate bags. Before leaving, he turned around and fed Psycho.

*****

Around the same time that Tre pulled up to Battlefield Park, Nice and Tommy pulled up as well. They exited their vehicles to conduct business.

"What's the deal, my nigs?" Tre greeted, giving them both handshakes and brotherly hugs. He then handed them two bags containing six bricks, three for Tommy, three for Nice. Tommy and Nice both tucked the work in their vehicles while Tre busted open a vanilla Dutch master.

After the drugs were tucked safely away, Tre started hitting them with some street knowledge. "Listen, y'all know I got love for y'all, right? And I know y'all will be on point with shit, but we have to step our game up a notch if we think we're going to be ahead of the game." Tre schooled them, passing the Dutch master filled with weed.

"Word is bond, I was thinking the same thing," Tommy spoke.

"You know what time I'm on, once I dump them three bricks, I'm grabbing like twenty pounds of that dumb shit. Speaking of dumb shit, Tre, where you get this tasty bud from?" Nice asked, exhaling some of that purple haze.

"I got it from this arrogant Jamaican nigga I know," Tre replied with a smirk on his face.

"Damn yo, you have to put me down with him, 'cause he got some fire," stated Nice, knowing the taste of his own weed.

"Y'all steady breathing on each other. I'm wondering if I can buzz too," Tommy intervened as he reached out for the blunt.

Off in the distance, a vehicle was approaching at a slow speed. Nice took notice of the white Crown Victoria as well as the others.

"Yo, I think this is the Po-Po," Nice blurted out.

Tre and Tommy both focused in on the Crown Victoria as it came to a halt. The driver side window rolled down.

"Damn, Tre, you look like you seen a ghost," C-low stated, leaning slightly out of the window.

"Man, we thought you was the police riding up in that car," Tre sighed in relief.

"Come on now, Tre, you know you have to ride like they ride to survive in this game," C-low said, exiting the vehicle. Tre gave Tommy and Nice some daps, letting them know he had some business to handle with C-low. Once they were out of earshot, Tre focused his attention back on C-low. "So you think you ready for this?

"I was born ready," he assured him. After Tre schooled him to what was going down, he gave him the bricks and they parted their separate ways.

CHAPTER 9: MONEY TIME

The next morning, C-low was inside of Pop's row house, sitting at a round wooden table along with his crew. C-low wasn't what you called your average hustler; he didn't get involved unless it was extremely beneficial. The bricks Tre just hit him off with was well worth his time. That was the main reason he called his crew to this meeting in the first place. Things were about to do a one-eighty turn for him. He just wanted to make sure everybody was on the same page. Scanning the prodigies carefully, C-low believed he had some of the best young goons one could have working for him. Trying to get comfortable in the wooden chair he was glued to, he thought about how life was going to be once the coke hit the streets. Reaching in his Jansport backpack, C-low exposed two bricks of cocaine. Placing it down on the table for his crew to get a better view, he studied their demeanor.

"I'm sure y'all know what y'all are looking at, right?" C-low said as he placed his hands on top of the bricks.

"What's that, heroin?" one of the young goons asked.

"No stupid. It's cocaine," another yelled.

"You're right, Bush. It is cocaine. You seem to be on point with your shit. That's why you're my lil homie," C-low praised him. The other young goon felt stupid for not knowing and was mad as hell that Bush knew. He only dealt with crack cocaine, so seeing powdery substance he assumed it was heroin.

"Listen good, we got here some of that fish scale shit. And for those that don't know what that means, it means we got some good ass coke. And after Pop's gets his hands on it, Lord knows what type of crack he's going to create. But no matter how good the work is, we only want to make twelve hundred off of each ounce. I want all competition knocked out of the box in the surrounding areas." C-low explained, looking at their faces hoping he made himself clear.

"What about them niggas down on 3rd street?" one of the young goons blurted out.

"What about them niggas? They better get in where the fuck they fit in!" C-low snarled, eyeing the goon with a stern look. "Now, is there any other worries?" he continued, not liking the last remark.

"Nah, let's get this money!" Bush yelled.

With that said, C-low grabbed both of the bricks from off the table and passed them to Pops. Pops was a chemist when it came to cooking up cocaine. If you wanted your street blocks flooded with customers, Pops was your man for the job. In his late fifties, Pops had seen it all. He was that been-there-done-that type of guy, always trying to school the young crowd. Pops used to get major money and party with some of the sexiest females back in the day. Until one day, he came home to find out someone had robbed him and murdered the love of his life. Ever since that dreadful day he's been using all sorts of drugs to smooth his worries and regrets.

"Do what you do Pops" C-low said, after passing him the bricks.

"Don't worry about shit, young blood. I'm going to put that '89 whipped game to it. Mothafuckas will be kicking down doors to get some of this shit," Pops assured him before walking off towards the kitchen.

Several hours and two six-packs of natural ice later, Pops was finally finished. C-low couldn't believe his eyes; Pops had just turned two bricks into ninety-two ounces. By the looks of things, Pops had it looking like some straight up butter as they used to call it back in the day.

"That shit looks like some ol' school butter, but is it that butter?" C-low questioned.

"Well, let's just see, young blood. Pass me the truth over there," Pops demanded, referring to his custom-made crack pipe. Placing a nice-sized amount in it, he flicked at the Bic lighter a few times before a large flame appeared. All you could hear was sizzling and popping sounds as he inhaled the crack cocaine. Pops eyes were wide open as he held in the evil drug, while a tingling sensation moved all over his body.

"So, what do you think?" C-low inquired.

Pops said nothing. All he could do was hold up his two thumbs.

"Boy, boy, we got us a kicker. This nigga got locked jaws," C-low announced with excitement. After doing his math in his head really quick, C-low figured if he made twelve-hundred off of each ounce, he would easily clear one hundred and ten thousand dollars. This was going to be a sweet come-up for him because he only owed Tre ninety-six thousand back. Plus, he still had two more bricks on tuck for insurance.

"Young blood, you think I can get some more of that shit?" Pops finally managed to talk.

"Shit, Pops, you can get whatever you like," C-low replied before reaching for his cell phone. Things were definitely about to be jumping. He just hoped everything moved fast enough for him. After breaking the crew off with the proper amount, he tucked the rest.

*****

Back in Atlanta, things couldn't have been better for Linda. A week had passed and she was spending money like crazy. Driving down Peachtree, she was styling and profiling in her new red CLK 550 drop-top convertible. Heading towards Lenox Square Mall, Linda had no idea that she was being tailed. Making a left into Lenox Square Mall's parking lot, she parked. In the distance, Fat Cat's worker was stalking his prey.

Three and a half hours later, Linda came sauntering out of the mall with her hands full with bags from Neiman & Marcus and Saks Fifth Avenue. Walking with no care in the world, she popped the trunk to her car. After placing the last bag in the trunk, she felt the presence of someone behind her. Before she was able to turn all the way around, she was shoved into the trunk of her own car. Not knowing what the hell was going on, she screamed for her life. Linda tried her best to fight her way up out of the trunk. As she was hit with the butt of the worker's gun, darkness swallowed her life, a full eclipse.

"Dumb bitch," Fat Cat's worker snarled, snatching the keys from her hand and closing the trunk.

CHAPTER 10: THERE'S ALWAYS A WEAK LINK

"Ahhh!" Linda screamed as Ricky poured gasoline over her wounds.

"Bitch, I'm tired of playing games!" Ricky bawled out. "Who was involved and where the fuck is my money?"

He'd been torturing her for over an hour with small cuts all over her body. Fat Cat's worker definitely came through; too bad he was lying dead next to Linda. When it came to his money, Ricky played no games with nobody.

Fading in and out, Linda was a trooper, but the pain she was experiencing was unbearable.

"If you tell me where the money is and who's involved, I promise to let you go," Ricky assured her.

Holding her head up high, she gazed into his evil eyes. She wished she had a gun so she could put a bullet in his sadistic head. But she was in a lose-lose situation. The only thing she could do was try to convince him to spare her life. Magic's name was what she blurted out, "He...he...he had his peoples from Delaware in on it," she muttered through swollen lips.

"And you're going to tell me how to find this Magic mothafucka?" Ricky asked, holding up her head.

"Yes," she replied, feeling defeated.

After receiving the information that he needed from her, Ricky gave her a smile from ear to ear, Miami style.

*****

It was now well over a half of million in cash Tre had piled up in his safe. The past few weeks had been really good for him. C-low had finished off the work so fast that he had to buy the other three bricks off of Nice. Nice was happy to come up off the work due to the fact that cocaine wasn't his line of work. Tre hadn't talked to Magic since the day he made it back home. He'd been trying to contact him for the past couple of days. Tre was in search for some more of that down south finest cocaine. While petting Psycho, Tre snapped to himself, "Damn, this nigga's still not returning any of my phone calls."

Too bad Tre wouldn't be able to get his hands on some more of that down south cocaine, or get in touch with Magic for that matter. All sorts of thoughts were traveling through Tre's mind. But he knew how his cousin was and knowing Magic, he was probably somewhere tricking. Too bad he was chasing a lost cause, now that Magic was somewhere floating with the fish. Tre's last hope was Tommy and his cocaine connect from up New York.

******

Disguised like a crack head, Detective Smith had been keeping tabs on C-low and his crew for the past couple of days. Smith observed them moving heavy amounts of drugs all of a sudden. C-low and his crew hadn't been moving sloppy or anything; it's just that they had been making too much money and not paying their taxes. Well, it was tax time and Uncle Smith wanted his cut.

Detective Smith was known as a big-time crooked cop. He would rob you blind and still charge you with something. If you didn't pay the way you weighed, then you were in the way.
As he exited his Crown Victoria, he noticed how smooth C-low's operation was moving. He approached a young goon from behind.

"Are you working?" Detective Smith asked, doing his best junkie impersonation, scratching at his chest.

"Yeah, what you looking for?" the goon asked.

"Me and my friend is looking for two one-hundred pieces."

"Man, I'll give you twenty-eight dimes for two-hundred dollars," the goon told him.

"I'm cool with that," Smith replied.

"Where's yo friend at anyway?" the goon asked, scanning the surroundings.

"He's right over there in the alley," Detective Smith pointed. Knowing the young goon would take the bait, they walked towards the alleyway together. Once in the alley, the young goon became suspicious.

"Man, where's your peoples at?!"

Instantly, Detective Smith swiveled around into action, landing a powerful punch into the goon's abdomen area.

"Aghh!" the young goon cried out in pain. The blow caused him to drop to one knee. Thinking it was a robbery, he tried reaching for his gun. But his attempts were too slow. Detective Smith was all over him. For Smith being in his early forties, he was still in excellent condition. He jabbed him in the stomach area once again, but this time with the goon's own gun.

"Aghh! Please, just take the drugs!" he begged. He was hoping one of his crew members would notice what was going on so they could come to his rescue.

"Shut the fuck up! I don't want no damn drugs, you young punk," he shouted back. He clearly saw the fear in his young eyes; the boy was terrified.

"You know, you're looking at a lot of time," Detective Smith said menacingly. "Drugs plus gun means a lot of fucking time, young punk."

Looking up in his attacker's eyes, the goon's fear changed to a different kind of fear.

"Listen, I can take you down right now for this alone and by the time you come back home, you wouldn't recognize the street," Smith threatened. "Or you can help me help you; it's your choice kid."

Smith had big plans in store for C-low and in order for his plans to come together he would need the young boy's help.

"What's your name, young punk?" Smith demanded.

"Bush," he croaked.

"Well, Bush, call me in two days," said Smith. He handed him his business card. "If you don't, I will find you and it will be a lot worse next time."

Smith exited the alleyway. Bush did the same minutes later, still holding his stomach. The block lieutenant strolled over to him.

"What the fuck is wrong with you?" the lieutenant asked.

"Nothing, man, I think I have the stomach virus," Bush lied, hoping his lie wasn't too easily noticed.

"Well, you need to get that fixed," the lieutenant said. "You know damn well you can't be out here like that. If C-low was to see you like this, he would have a fit."

With that, Bush was on his way thinking about the fucked-up situation he'd gotten himself into.

*****

Up in one of his stash spots on Van Buren Street, between 2nd and 3rd streets, C-low was counting the money his crew had made so far for the day. In a short period of time, C-low was now the man in his area, running eight blocks now that he was on the rise. To say each block was doing good was an understatement; they were booming with business.

C-low really had his shit well organized, from the runners on every corner to the lookouts posted on the roofs. His shit was air-tight in his eyes. On a bad day, each block was easily clearing twenty-five hundred, and on a good day, it could be anywhere between five to seven thousand dollars. And, if it just so happened to be the first or the fifteenth, the usual pay days; well, let's just say the sky was the limit.

The money was coming in like clockwork, which boosted C-low's ego by the minute. He felt like he was Ace, Alpo, and Rich Porter all in one from his favorite movie, 'Paid in Full.' But just as good as things were flowing, there was also the bad. Damn near each week, C-low had to make an example out of a fool. Not to mention, just this morning he had to pistol whip some hustler for trying to make money on one of his blocks. Out of the corner of his eyes, he watched as a young female wrapped the last rubber band around the wad of money.

"All finished," she said proudly, standing up and showing off her sexy curves.

"So are you ready for me to drop you off?" C-low asked, ready to get back to the handling business. "Like hell," she said, unbuttoning the top buttons of her Seven jeans. "You need to give me some of that sweet dick over there."

Although C-low was real strict when it came to his money, he couldn't resist her young beauty. He began to unbutton his own pants while signaling her to sit down on the couch. As he approached her, the young girl could clearly see the bulge growing right before her eyes.

Excited by his thickness, she wet her lips and began sucking and licking every inch of his shaft. C-low thought he was going to lose his mind the way she was sucking his manhood while playing with his balls at the same time.

"I see you like that, don't you?" the young girl teased while smacking his penis on her lips before engulfing it once again.

"I see you know a little som'em, som'em," he replied nonchalantly.

"A little som'em. Well let's see if you can handle this," she said seductively, placing her hands on his tight-ass cheeks. She started deep-throating him like an expert as the saliva dripped down the side of her mouth.

"God damn! That's it right there, girl!" he chanted, enjoying her head game. His dick jerked with excitement as it rested in the back of her throat. Satisfied with her work, she pulled down her Seven jeans exposing her sexy thighs and her booty-licious ass.

With her now positioned right, C-low got right into the swing of things, pulling her thong aside. As soon as he entered her warm zone, she gripped the top of the couch for support. Her juices began flowing down his legs like the Mississippi River, as he stroked in and out of her. Arching her back even more C-low dug in even deeper as he held onto her shoulders for better support.

"Damn!" he grunted, still stroking in and out.

"You like that? You... like... this... pussy," she said in pauses, making her ass cheeks bounce one at a time, still matching each stroke of his.

Turned on by her behavior, C-low pulled out and dove face first into her soaked pussy from the back. Playing with her clitoris with one hand and feasting on her pussy was driving her crazy.

"Aww... shit... baby! Right... there!" she moaned, enjoying every bit of it.

"Yeah, you like that?" he said, coming up for air then diving right back into her love hole.

"C-low! Oh... my... God! Oh... shit.... I'm about to cum!" she screamed, releasing what looked like a waterfall.

This was his cue. He slid right back into her with ease. Pounding away like a horny dog, he felt himself about to explode.

"Fuck!" he yelled as he reached the climax.

Picking up the pace, she yelled, "Yes, baby, cum all over my ass." And that's exactly what he did.

"Damn, girl, that was a mean shot there," he said, fixing himself to roll out. "But a nigga got some things to do."

"Figures," the young girl said, grabbing her things before they left.

CHAPTER 11: I DIDN'T KNOW HE HAD YOU LIKE THAT

Stepping out of the shower, Casina could hear the lyrics of Nikki Minaj playing. She dashed out of the bathroom towards her room. From the ring tone she heard, she knew it was Lolita calling. Snatching up her iPhone, she touched the answer box on the screen.

"What's up, Chicka?" Casina said.

"Don't 'what's up Chicka' me! What the hell is your problem? I haven't heard from you in a couple of days." Lolita snapped at her.

"Gurl, I've been so busy with school and all. All my time's been going to studying. It seems like that woman gives a test damn near every week. But it's finally over and now I can bre-"

"Good!" Lolita snapped in before she could even finish. "That means we can go out tonight, so be ready by eight o' clock. She hung up, not even giving Casina a chance to respond.

Damn, if I did have plans, they sure as hell would have been canceled, thought Casina, tossing her cell back on the bed. She took a deep breath and let out a long sigh. Her classes at the University of Miami were taking a toll on her. Taking more than two years off after her parent's death, she was finally in her junior year of college. With her finals approaching, Casina still couldn't shake Tre out of her mind.

Dropping her towel, she flopped down on the edge of her bed while reaching for her amber romance scented Victoria's Secret. Her hands rubbed down her soft legs with the lotion; all Casina could think about was the feelings and the intensity of that night she had spent with Tre. Just the thought of his lips and the way he had touched her was making her tunnel of love release its warm juices. Reaching her hand down to her pleasure spot, she started touching her clitoris, moving her pointer finger in a circular motion.

"Gurl, snap out of it! That sexy man has to have women throwing pussy at him all the time," she said out loud.

Casina's backside jiggled as she walked towards her dresser. She grabbed her pink-and-black lace bra with matching thong she had gotten from Frederick's of Hollywood. It was already 6:45 p.m. and she had no idea what she wanted to wear. The fact that Lolita didn't give her any idea of where they were going just made the task of getting dressed even more difficult.

Casina was the type of person who wanted to look her best at all times. She had a dress for any occasion and the perfect shoes to match them. Finally, after searching her closet a thousand times, she decided to don her little black Roberto Cavalli dress. It was the perfect freak'em dress for a night on the town or an elegant night at an upscale restaurant. The deep V-neck exposed her cleavage just right. Another detail she loved about this dress was the high waistband. It was bronze-trimmed with diamonds that set just below her breast. Her 4 1/2 inch ankle strap bronze Roberto Cavalli pumps harmonized with her little black dress to a 'T.' All fancy needed now was to grab her accessories to make her outfit complete. With an outfit so immaculate, her accessories couldn't be nothing less than her diamond choker with the matching earrings that her father had brought from Gray & Sons Jewelers. The set was a graduation present and would light up any room. When she placed the diamond choker around her neck, many emotional memories of her parents started to surface. Just as she was putting in her other earrings, her cell phone began to ring. Picking it up, she answered, "Hola, Chicka!"

"Hola to you, are you ready?" Lolita asked.

"Yes, gurl, and looking fabulous too!" she replied, checking herself out from side to side.

"Bitch, I didn't ask you that," replied Lolita, frowning.

"Don't hate," chuckled Casina. "Mind telling me where we are going?"

"We can talk about it on the way. Now come on, I'm out front."

"Alright, give me two seconds," Casina replied before disconnecting the call.

Lolita looked in awe as the front door swung open. Casina flounced towards Lolita's car.

"Look at this bitch," Lolita said out loud as Casina was getting in the car. "Damn, bitch, what's that, like a forty-thousand-dollar outfit you put together?"

"Nah, not really. Close but no. I caught the dress at a smoking price of thirty-five hundred. And we were together when I bought the shoes because they were on sale for one thousand and forty dollars, remember? And you know the jewelry my Dad bought for me; that was only twenty-nine thousand," Casina explained.

"Oh, so I was off by like six thousand. Excuse me." Lolita replied sarcastically.

"Whatever, Chicka. Do you mind telling me where we're going now?"

"Well, I kind of figured we could go to Brice's on the Ave and by the time we've finished there, something should be jumping off by then."

"Oh, that's what's up. I know you got our gurl up in here?" Casina asked, referring to Beyonce'.

"You know I do, gurl," she replied as she pulled off.

About an hour later...

Settled at the table, Lolita noticed that her girl had stopped eating and had drifted off into a deep train of thought.

"Hey, earth to Casina, gurl you okay?"

"Yeah, I'm cool," replied Casina, playing with her food.

"You don't look like you're cool. We gurls now; you know you can talk to me about anything," she said, meaning every word of it.

Trying to brush off her urge to talk about Tre, she lied. "I know, gurl, but for real, I'm cool. I just still have some school shit on my mind."

After dinner, the two of them headed towards South Beach. Once they arrived at their destination, the two partied like divas. Lolita could still tell that something was on Casina's mind more than some college stuff. So during the ride home, she hit Casina with a thousand questions.

"You think I'm dumb, don't you? You thinking about that nigga you met at the club from up north, ain't you?"

Casina looked at Lolita with a devilish grin and responded, "It's that noticeable?"

"Yeah," Lolita said. "Because, Casina, you haven't been yourself since we came back. That nigga must have been something else. You said he was sexy as hell but damn, I didn't know he had you like that. Especially all this time. How long has it been since we were up there?"

"It's been a minute, but it's something about him, Chicka," replied Casina. "I just can't stop thinking about him."

"Yeah, you're addicted to his ass. Gurl, you sure he didn't throw that dick on you?" Lolita questioned, tilting her head sideways.

"Please, I don't do those one night stands," Casina snapped. "It's deeper than that!" She was upset that her girl would think of her like that.

"Gurl, I was just playing with you," Lolita said. "Have you called him yet?"

"No, I'm scared," she replied, staring out the window.

Pulling up to the mansion, Lolita parked and turned towards Casina. "Scared of what?"

"Gurl, you know how Ricky and Rayman are. I'm scared he might be the one. Maybe he's the man I've been seeking for, but then they might do their usual and run him off. I just don't know, Chicka. I have a lot on my mind right now." After a long sigh, Casina continued. "Alright, gurl, thanks for the night out. I needed that. I'll call you tomorrow." she said as she opened the car door to get out.

"Okay, gurl," Lolita replied.

As Casina was walking up her walkway, she heard Lolita yell out. "Casina! You need to call him!" Casina continued walking towards her front door, never acknowledging that she heard what Lolita had yelled. Entering the residence, Casina passed her brother Ricky as if he didn't exist. Once upstairs, she stripped down and jumped in the shower. She could still hear Lolita's voice playing over and over in her head. "Casina, you need to call him."

Once out of the shower, she rubbed down her legs with her favorite Shea Butter lotion. With Tre still on her mind, she reached for her iPhone and scrolled down till she reached Tre's name. She tapped the green talk box on the screen and waited patiently for her call to be connected. "Please wait while your party is being located," she heard the automated system say. As she was waiting, Casina heard the song playing as his caller tone, "Call me, so I can make it juicy for you."

"Awh, that's my song," Casina stated, singing along. Right when she finished singing, his answering machine picked up.

"Leave a message," she heard a deep voice say and then Lil Wayne continued to play until the sound of the beep. After leaving a message, her heart skipped a beat when she heard his voice again. Just the sound of his vocals on the machine made her want him even more.

Back in Wilmington...

"You just come to see me when you want to see me all of a sudden, huh?" Sherry asked.

"Better late than never," Tre responded, admiring her wearing nothing but a pair of black lace panties and a pair of black stilettos. Sherry attacked him like a kid attacks candy, pulling out his manhood. The way she worked her magic, his body responded with excitement and anxious anticipation. While Tre was leaving a message all over her face, a person that he had been waiting to hear from was leaving a message on his cell phone.

The next morning after checking his messages, Tre was speechless. "Damn, fucking with Sherry ass," he thought while hitting the talk button on the cell phone. After a few rings, Casina answered, "Hello?"

"Hey, can I speak to Casina, please?" said Tre.

"This is she. Who's calling?" she replied, knowing who it was.

"I'm pretty sure you know that answer already," he said with a charming voice.

"Yeah, I know who this is," said Casina, disappointed. "This is the same person I called last night but all I got was a voicemail."

"Well, is there anything I can do to make it up to you?"

"Hmm... maybe I can come up with something."

"Well, think fast, 'cause I was planning on coming down there in two weeks to see you."

"Don't get me all excited. I'll believe it when I see it."

"Say no more. I guess we will just have to see, then," he said. After two more hours of conversation, Casina hung up with Tre on her mind like crazy now. Lost in her own thoughts, she heard her phone ring, snapping her out of her daze. She rushed to answer it. It was Lolita.

"Damn," she thought to herself. She wasn't even finished getting dressed yet. "Hola, Chicka," she answered, still getting herself together.

"Bitch, tell me you ready?" barked Lolita.

"Gurl, my fault. I just got off the phone with him, gurl," she responded with a smile on her face.

"Who?" Lolita inquired.

"Tre! That's who." Casina let it be known.

"Well, bitch, you can tell me about that phone call while we're shopping."

"I don't know what's the rush," said Casina, putting on her jeans.

"You know we have to be the first bitches in Miami with that new shit."

Laughing at her friend, Casina said, "Okay." Within minutes, they were off ready to enjoy their shopping spree.

CHAPTER 12: A WEEKEND IN PARADISE

That past two weeks had been flying for Casina. She maneuvered in and out of traffic in her platinum drop-top Aston Martin DB9, heading towards Miami International Airport. She bobbed her head to the lyrics of Trina's new hit. As she approached the front of the airport, Casina noticed Tre standing there as if he was modeling for a magazine cover. Just the sight of his dark chocolate complexion, wavy hair, and sexy lips made her love cave drool. Not to mention he was styling in the latest threads.

"Damn, this chick pulls up in an Aston Martin," Tre thought as Casina hopped out to greet him.

She was wearing a Gucci tank top, linen shorts, and a pair of Gucci platform sandals.

"I guess you're a man of your word," she replied, giving him a hug.

"You haven't seen anything yet." He hugged and held her in his arms. Breaking his gaze, Casina popped the trunk for him to place his luggage in. Tre then went to the driver's side to open the door for her.

"Thank you," she said, getting in.

"You're welcome," he replied, showing off his pearly whites. Once inside, Casina turned back up the music as the two bobbed their heads to the lyrics while heading towards the hotel.

*****

"Excuse me, I have reservations under Tremane Money."

"Yes, sir," the receptionist typed in the computer. "What type of room did you reserve?"

"A king suite," he replied.

"I'm sorry, sir, but we're out of king suites. But for the inconvenience, we can upgrade your suite to a deluxe suite with no extra charge."

"Okay, I'll take it," Tre replied with relief.

"But sir, there will be a two hour delay on that room due to housekeeping," she informed him, making the corrections in the computer.

"Damn, you mean to tell me I have to wait?" Tre asked, looking from the receptionist to Casina.

"What are we going to do for the two hours?"

"We can go to Wet Willy's," suggested Casina.

"Wet Willy's? I'm not trying to get wet, sweetheart," Tre replied, confused.

"You're not gonna get wet silly. Come on," Casina replied, pulling him from the lobby.

*****

Twenty minutes later, Tre and Casina were outside of Wet Willy's. Tre felt stupid, now knowing that Wet Willy's was a restaurant and not a water park. Once inside, Tre was shocked by all the beautiful women standing before him. He had never seen so many eye-catching women in his life. But still with all the exotic women present, none of them could touch Casina's beauty. As the waiter seated them to an outside booth, all eyes were on the two.

"Can I get you anything to drink?" the waiter asked.

"Yes, we would like two 'Call a Cab' drinks please," Casina said, turning back to Tre.

"So, Tre, how do you like Miami so far?"

"It's cool, but since I'm with you, it's Paradise," Tre replied, making her blush.

"Here you go, miss and sir," the waiter reappeared, placing the tropical drinks in front of them.

"Thank you," Tre said.

"Would you two like anything else?" the waiter asked.

"Are you hungry?" Casina asked Tre.

"Not really," he replied.

"Can you just give us a large order of butterfly shrimp, please?" By the time the shrimp was brought to them, Tre had already had two 'Call a Cab' drinks.

"Excuse me, do you have anything other than these water-ice type of drinks?" Tre asked the waiter.

"Sir, these are our top sellers," said the waiter. "But we do have stronger drinks. Would you like 'Super Man'?"

"You sure you want that?" interjected Casina. "That drink is real strong, you know," said Casina.

"These fruity drinks can't tell me nothing," said Tre.

"Suit yourself," she replied, sipping from her straw.

Two 'Super Man' drinks later, Tre was passed grooving, and Casina could clearly see that. "I think the suite should be ready by now," she said.

"I think you're right. These damn Super Man's done crept up on a brotha," Tre responded, trying to get himself together.

*****

As the two entered the suite, they were amazed by the luxury. The style of it was very light and elegant. Walking further into the suite, they noticed three couches to the left by the balcony, a mini bar sat directly in the middle of the suite, and a bathroom was off to the right. Through double doors inside, there sat a king-sized bed and a Jacuzzi in the middle of the room with another balcony. Tre was so busy admiring the view from the balcony that he didn't notice Casina putting on her Michael Kors bathing suit. Lost in his own thoughts, Tre was startled by the sound of running water filling up in the large sized Jacuzzi. He turned around ogling at the beauty that stood in front of him. *Damn, I'm lucky*, he thought to himself.

"Are you going to just stand there and stare, or are you going to join me?" Casina said with a grin, climbing into the Jacuzzi.

"I only have to be told once, beautiful," he replied, undressing.

As she watched him without clothes, she saw how his demeanor was laid back, smooth, and calculated. Casina ran her eyes all over his body, noticing how much his body was ripped with muscles. Not to mention his tattoos and his perfect six-pack. Ignoring the stares, Tre climbed into the Jacuzzi. The heat from the water intensified the alcohol level and it had him on cloud nine. At that very moment, Tre didn't want anything but Casina. His thoughts had his mind racing. Her skin felt like silk as his leg brushed across hers. Feeling the love monster growing between his legs, Tre fantasized about what Casina's insides would feel like. As they locked eyes, Casina felt the desire burning between her thighs as well.

"I want you," she softly spoke.

Caught off guard, Tre was speechless. Leading the way, she exited the Jacuzzi while slowly strutting towards the bed. Stretched across the bed, she spread her enticing legs so that he could remove her bathing suit.

Slowly and gently, he flipped her on her stomach. Tracing her body with his finger, he started giving her back bites. As she gripped hold of the sheets, she begged for more while arching her back like a professional. With her face in the pillow, Tre feasted on her love cave. Unable to control herself, Casina moaned for more as Tre moved his tongue in and out of her, making her shake and tremble. It was as if he wrote a book on pussy-eating. Before Tre knew it, she climaxed, releasing her warm juices everywhere.

Admiring his work, she turned around and started passionately kissing him. Tre then climbed on top of her, and parted her sea with his ship. She jumped from the size of his love monster at first. But once mother nature kicked in, she grabbed his back and pulled him in closer. The closer she pulled him in, the deeper he went. She begged him not to stop. Scooping his hands under her ass cheeks, Tre drove in and out like a porn star. Casina couldn't believe how good he was making her feel; had it been that long or was he just that damn good?

Turning her over, he was loving her Brazilian ass while making love to her backside. It felt just the way he imagined it would, amazing. Casina buried her head back into the pillow, enjoying the feeling of his shaft up inside of her. With her back arched, Tre was knee deep in her. Stroking away, the sounds of sex could be heard. At the point of no return, Tre pulled out and released a heavy load. Tre was now enjoying Paradise as he held Casina in his arms.

For the rest of the weekend, Tre and Casina were all over Miami. Enjoying the time they spent together, Tre made sure they lived it up to the fullest. There was so much they had found out about each other that you would have thought they knew each other for years.

Pulling up to the Airport, Casina parked and faced Tre.

"Thank you for coming and thank you so much for the beautiful time we shared together."

"You're saying it as if I wasn't coming back," Tre replied, lifting her chin to gaze into her eyes. Looking deep into her eyes, Tre had seen an untold story he was dying to know.

"I will see you again soon," he assured her, before kissing her like couples do on prom night.

Casina's world was on pause as Tre exited the vehicle, leaving her mind racing....

CHAPTER 13: HERE WE GO AGAIN

"We got that hard white that will keep yo body up all night!" Bush yelled. He was posted up in the middle of 2nd street.

Ever since his encounter with Detective Smith weeks ago, Bush had relocated to a different block trying his best to avoid him. Bush had been out all morning making a killing. He watched as a junkie approached him. It looked like she was taken right out of a Michael Jackson's video 'Thriller.'

"A' Bush, give me a twenty," she said.

"I'm not taking no shorts today, Curl King. Straight money for real," he replied, reaching inside the front part of his pants to retrieve his stash of drugs.

"I got eighteen. Please let me slide for two dollars," Curl King voiced, scratching at her chest.

"Damn, I've been out here too all morning."

"Here, with yo beggin' ass," he replied frustrated, shoving her the twenty bag of crack and snatching the money.

Curl King got halfway down the block when Bush realized that she had given him only fifteen dollars.

"A' Curl King! You short bitch!" Bush yelled, holding up the money.

Curl King sung aloud and picked up her pace, "I don't want to be a crack head no more. I'm not a crack head, I just smoke a lot." She took off around the corner. There was no point in chasing her because one thing is for sure and two things are for certain; you're not catching no crack head.

Twenty minutes later, Bush was finished with his shift. Hopping in his car, he was now on his way to meet up with a female he met last night at the Chinese store. Stopping at the traffic light, Bush was bobbing his head to a new Southern Smoke mixed CD. Looking towards his left, he noticed a Crown Vic pulling alongside him. Thinking nothing of it, he continued to bob his head. The light turned green and Bush was now searching for his weed. He spotted the sack of weed on the passenger side floor. Keeping the steering wheel straight, he reached down quickly and grabbed the sack of weed. Looking back up, he was startled by flashing red and blue lights.

"Fuck! If it ain't one thing it's another!" he barked out loud, trying his hardest to stuff the sack of weed into the seat. The Crown Vic was now behind him, pulling him over. Knowing that he had finished off all the crack that he had on him, he really wasn't tripping off of the police being behind him. The weed that he'd just stuffed didn't bother him at all, 'cause after all, it was only weed.

After pulling over, Bush reached in his glove box for his license, registration, and insurance info. When he looked back towards the window, his heart dropped instantly. It was Detective Smith.

"So, you were going to keep avoiding me, right?" Detective Smith shouted.

"N-No man, I was going to get at you," Bush replied, nervous as hell.

"You think I'm some rookie or som'em," Smith barked. "You know what it is and you know what I'm capable of. I want to know who is supplying y'all and where the stash house is at. And I want to know this sooner than later. Understood?

"Alright, man."

Noticing some onlookers, Detective Smith tried to cover up his plan so that no one would look at Bush suspiciously. "This is a warning! But next time I catch you speeding, I will lock your ass up!" he yelled, loud enough for the spectators and walked back to his car. Knowing that he couldn't shake the situation, Bush knew what he had to do.

Detective Smith was growing impatient with Bush. His young goons weren't doing well with the last product he gave them. And, with C-low flooding the west side of the city, his situation wasn't any better. "This fucking kid needs to make this happen, or his black ass is through," he was thinking, noticing a young lady standing on the corner. Smith tucked his badge and pulled over.

"What's shaking, daddy?" the young prostitute asked, approaching this vehicle.

"Get in and find out," Detective Smith replied, eyeing her.

Once inside the car, the young prostitute became nervous. This was her first client on the streets, and she wasn't used to dating like this.

"How much you charging?" Smith asked.

"Twenty for head, fifty dollars to fuck," she replied, rubbing his inner thigh.

"Well, how about I get a free sample or your ass is going to jail," Smith calmly stated, exposing his badge.

"Fuck! You the po-po?" she replied, feeling played.

"Come on and stop wasting time. You know what to do," he said, leaning his seat back and unzipping his pants. Feeling angry, but in a lose-lose situation, the young prostitute did what she did best and pulled out his little penis.

*****

It was jam-packed at Kingswoods Park. The sun was beaming and the females were scheming. Hustlers and wannabe hustlers from all over the inner city came out to show love for the female softball games. Some came to see the females sweating in their little shorts. Others wanted people to sweat them. And as always, the stick-up kids were out lurking, looking for a quick come-up.

The second game was just about to start when Tre pulled up in his new black Range Rover Sport with smoke-grey interior. Complementing his Range Rover, his Asanti Luxury Grille package shined as did his twenty-four inch Asanti rims. Behind him was Tommy stunting in his all-white Lincoln Navigator and Nice was shining in his black Escalade ESV; both cars were sitting on chrome. All eyes were on them as they exited their vehicles. As Nice hopped out of his truck, he popped his hatch back and the song 'Ten Commandments' by the late rapper Biggie Smalls filled the air.

"A' Shelly Mack, ain't that yo peoples Tre?" Kris said, pointing in the direction of the blaring music.

Following her hand, Shelly Mack spotted her cousin. "That's him," she confirmed. After grabbing her hot sausage and soda from Heavy's Food Stand, Shelly Mack strutted over to Tre with Kris in tow.

"Whas'up cuz?" Shelly Mack said, biting into her hot sausage.

"You," Tre replied.

"I see you riding big now," she responded, admiring his new Range Rover.

"You think big, you ride big," he schooled her.

Just then their conversation got interrupted by the lyrics of Jim Jones' hit song, 'We Fly High' blasting from behind them.

"A' Tre, what's really good?" the voice from behind said.

Turning around, Tre noticed C-low sitting in a silver-and-black Maserati Quattroporte.

"Damn, my nig, you should've been in that video with Jim Jones and them," said Tre, giving C-low some daps. "What's that, about a hundred thousand dollars? Did that shit even hit the streets yet?"

"Man, this shit ain't nothing," C-low replied. "I got it next to nothing from my peoples Ace from out of Bad News VA."

"What, he got a car lot or som'em?" Tre asked, looking at the car.

"Nah, he got a chop shop. If he don't have what you want, he can get what you want," C-low assured him.

"Say word, you know you got to plug me in on that one."

"You know I got you, but on the real, I'm gonna need some more work at the end of the week. This shit is moving like crazy."

"Oh, so this the man we've been getting our work from?" Bush blurted out from behind.

Turning around, C-low glared at Bush like he was fucking crazy. "Some people need to close their mouth and let their ears do the talking," he said, turning his attention back at Tre. Studying Bush's demeanor, Tre wasn't feeling his vibe. It was just something about him that didn't sit well with him. He just couldn't put his finger on it.

"We'll rap about it later," Tre said before walking off.

Halfway through the softball game, Tre was enjoying himself when a commotion between two goons broke out.

"Fuck you, nigga!" the skinny goon yelled, jumping up in the other goon's face.

"Nah nigga, fuck you!" the short chubby goon retorted, backing away and pulling out his gun at the same time.

"POP! POP! POP! POP!" Shots rang out and screams filled the air.

"Yo, son! We out!" Tommy yelled, pulling out his .50 caliber gun.

"Hold up, where's my peoples at?" Tre asked, scanning the park. Looking to his far right, he spotted Shelly Mack squatted behind the car with her .380 handgun out.

"Girl! Bring yo ass on!" Tre shouted.

Jumping up, Shelly Mack yelled to her friend to come on as they jumped in the Range Rover with Tre.

"What about my car?" Shelly Mack protested.

"Fuck that, we will get it later," replied Tre.

Niggas, Tre thought as he pulled off with Tommy and Nice behind him.

*****

The next day at Battlefield Park, Tre was shooting some hoops with Psycho present. The sun was out and the temperature was in the mid-eighties. The few bystanders that were there stayed their distance in fear of the pit bull by Tre's side. On the bench a few young girls sat with excitement and lust as they watched the sweat drip down his back and six-pack. Looking in their direction, the young girls had no shame as they continued to stare and giggle. The way they were dressed was begging for attention. Tre knew if he was ten years younger, he would have given them the attention they wanted. Smiling at them, Tre went back to shooting more shots.

After a while, Tre looked up and spotted Tommy's Navigator pulling up. Tommy had Jay-Z lyrics thumping from his 'Kingdom Come' album. Tre was nodding his head as he approached the truck.

Tommy jumped out to greet his homie. "This nigga Jay-Z is a fuckin' genius, son," Tommy stated, giving Tre a brotherly handshake and hug.

"Who you telling? Hands down, that nigga is the best that ever done it," replied Tre, spinning the ball on one of his fingers.

"Yeah but, son, don't forget about Biggie and Tupac," Tommy said, leaning up against his truck as he broke open a vanilla Dutch.

"Man, real talk, everybody's talking about Tupac and Biggie, who the best this, who the best that," explained Tre.

"No disrespect, but they both dead. Biggie wasn't in the game long enough, even though he made an impact while he had his run. But that nigga only dropped like four albums, I think. And Tupac, yes he was the shit, and it didn't matter how you was feeling; you could always pop a Tupac CD in and could relate to it. But neither of them was on Jay-Z's level. You know why? 'Cause they didn't do half the shit they spit about. Biggie was rapping about other hustlers' lives and Tupac didn't start living that life until he became successful. Now tell me that ain't ass backwards. Now Jigga is the truth. That nigga said, 'I come into the game a hundred grand strong, nine to be exact, from grinding g-packs.' Now see that shit right there is some hard shit," Tre finished.

"Son, what makes you think that shit he was spitting was the truth? That shit could have been lies, yo."

"We both can agree Jay-Z is the icon of Hip Hop, right? We also can agree that a lot of people be targeting Jay-Z 'cause their own name is in the rap game. Now, when have they ever come out of their mouths saying that any of the shit Hov be spitting was false? Come on now, name one person." Tre paused. "See, you can't. Hov's credibility was always on point."

"You right, son. I never looked at it like that. But I still love Biggie. That nigga says some hard shit too," Tommy stated, passing the blunt.

"Biggie that nigga too. I agree with that. But on the real, whas'up with yo peoples from up-top? This nigga C-low is running through this shit like it's nothing."

"I know. I need some more my damn self. That nigga Mar ran through that shit as well. I'ma holla at my peps and get some prices."

"That's whas'up," said Tre. "Just make sure that shit is proper. 'Cause we can't go from grade A to some bullshit."

"Son, I ain't new to this. I'm true to this," replied Tommy, pounding on his chest.

"I know you will handle it big, homie," Tre retorted, passing back the blunt.

"Damn, you might as well keep that small ass shit. I guess the puff, puff, pass rule don't apply to you," Tommy said, looking down at the small piece of blunt in Tre's hand.

"My bad, dawg, you know how it is when a brotha gets to talking too much."

"Well, the blunts and the weed is right there," Tommy replied, encouraging him to roll up another blunt.

"WOOF! WOOF! WOOF! WOOF!" Psycho barked. Turning in that direction, the two noticed a city squad car passing.

"Yeah, you see that shit? Even my dog hates the police," Tre stated proudly.

"Son, when you going to mate him? Word the motha, I know mad niggas who would want a pup."

"I don't know, yo. Maybe next year."

Feeling the vibration on his hip, Tommy realized his cell phone was going off. "This that nigga Mar now," he said, holding up his phone.

"Well, handle your B-I, my nig," Tre replied, giving him a hand dap.

"Alright, yo. I'm going to handle that for us too."

Patting on his leg, Tre signaled Psycho to come on. He was tired, sweaty, and in need of a shower. Hopping in his Range Rover, he popped in 50 Cent's album. The lyrics of '21 Questions' filled the air.

"If I fell off tomorrow, would you still love me?" Tre continued to rap while thinking about his weekend with Casina. A female like Casina didn't have to be a gold digger. But Tre knew she wasn't going to chill with a broke dude either.

CHAPTER 14: SHE'S ON SOME BULLSHIT

"I've called this asshole a million times, and he's still not answering his damn phone!" Sherry shouted, throwing down her T-Mobile.

"Ouchh!!! Gurl, you sewing it in too tight. Bitch, I'm not Tre. Please don't take it out on me," Sherry's friend said.

"You right, gurl. I'm sorry," Sherry replied. She had been frustrated and it was beginning to show. Sherry was just tired of being lonely. The one man she wanted to be with so badly, didn't want to be with her.

"You know what, I need to take my ass out tonight and have a good time," she thought to herself.

"Nye, you trying to go out tonight with me?" Sherry asked, sewing in her last piece of track.

"Gurl, I don't know. My mans be trippin'. I got to see what this fool is doing first," Nye replied.

"Well, let me know, 'cause I'm going out tonight to shake my ass," Sherry said, handing her friend a mirror.

*****

Checking his cell phone, Tre noticed Sherry calling for the tenth time. Since this weekend he'll be in Miami, Florida, Tre had been avoiding her phone calls. If it wasn't money on his mind, it was Casina. Tre was sitting back scanning his apartment. A lot had changed over the past two months.

"I guess it's true what they say; you can be broke one day and rich the next," Tre thought aloud, reaching for the Nike book bag of money that C-low had given him. After counting it, Tre couldn't believe the type of money C-low was making.

"Damn, he's turning his blocks into gold mines," he continued reflecting as he placed the fifty thousand dollars into the safe along with the rest of his stash money. "I'm going to need a bigger safe," he said to himself.

"WOOF! WOOF! WOOF!" Psycho barked as he darted out of the bedroom towards the front room. Tre grabbed his chrome .44 magnum with the infrared from under the mattress before heading towards the door.

"Who is it?" he asked, looking through the peephole.

"It's me," an older woman's voice said.

Noticing it was his neighbor, Maggie Bell, Tre tucked his .44 magnum into his waistband. Glancing down at Psycho, he signaled him to calm down before opening the door.

"I thought you might want this," Maggie Bell said, handing him some of her freshly baked deep dish sweet potato pie. Maggie Bell was a sweet old lady who would always give Tre a plate of her soul food. Numerous times Tre would try to give her money for bills, but she would kindly refuse to take it. Tre didn't know his father or his mother but as soon as he graduated, Maggie Bell filled that void the minute he met her when she moved across the hall.

"Thank you so much Ms. Maggie Bell," Tre said, giving her a kiss on the cheek.

"You're welcome, child," she replied before walking back across the hall.

As soon as Tre closed the door, his cell phone chirped. Picking up his Boost Mobile, Tre pushed the button.

"Whas'up, Nice?" Tre answered.

"I can't call it. You trying to go out tonight?"

"Where's it jumping at?" asked Tre.

"Club Ecstasy's. It's going to be poppin' tonight."

"I guess so. What time?"

"We'll meet there around eleven o'clock tonight," said Nice.

"Cool. I'll meet y'all there," he replied before ending the call. After he hung up, Tre started digging into his deep dish sweet potato pie. Working on his second piece, Tre's other cell phone started to ring. Looking at the screen, he noticed it was Casina. Hitting the talk button, Tre walked off towards his bedroom.

*****

The outside of Ecstasy's Night Club looked like any other club would look on a Thursday night...live. If you were to ride by, you would see some of the sharpest guys and some of the finest females standing in line. All were waiting to get in one of Wilmington's hottest nightclubs. Inside, Tre was being stalked by Sherry's ogle-eyes. He caught sight of her looking at him, but didn't pay her any mind. He had been getting tired of the way she had been acting lately.

"Home chick stalking, ain't she?" Nice asked over the loud music.

"Man, I ain't stunnin' her. She be tripping like a nigga owe her or som'em," Tre replied, sipping his double shot of Remy.

"Whas'up, cousin?" Shelly Mack shouted out, walking up from behind him. She was brown-skinned, cute in the face and small in the waist. She had one of them skinny bubble asses, with a Jada Pinkett swagger from off the movie 'Low Down Dirty Shame.'

"You shittin' on them tonight, ain't you?" Tre stated, checking out her attire. Shelly Mack had on a short sleeved gold-and-cream fitted t-shirt. A pair of Tru Religion skinny jeans showed off her well-stocked ass, and a pair of gold Givenchy heels. The highlights in her hair was killing them as well.

"You know I'm a hood star, but look at you, I know these broads sweatin' you," she replied, placing her hands on her hips. "Well, hood star, what you drinking on?" Tre asked, laughing at his little cousin.

"Come on, Tre, you know we pop bottles of Rosé 'cause the crew is never cheap," Shelly Mack rhymed, trying to rap.

Thirty minutes later, Tre, Nice, and Tommy were outside on the deck, flicking it up big time. Tommy was drawing a lot of attention with his iced-out chain and its enormous charm.

"How much?" Tre asked, checking out the pictures before him.

"They seven dollars a pieces," the photographer said, placing the pictures into the paper frames.

"Y'all took ten, so just give me fifty dollars."

Tre pulled out the cash. "Here goes a hundred and eighty. Give us three copies each."

"Thanks. If y'all ever need my services, and I mean ever, here's my card." Tre read the business card. It said, 'Lookin' Good Photos.'

Back inside the club, they were enjoying themselves. DJ Khaled was thumping through the speakers with his smashing hit 'I'm So Hood.' Lowering the music, DJ Breeze came through the speakers.

"Big ups to Tre, Nice, and Tommy. We see you niggas." DJ Breeze turned the music back up.

The party was coming to an end and the parking lot was booming. It looked like a car show; guys were trying their hardest to show off their whips. The guys were trying to creep off and the females were trying to freak off.

Tre never saw Sherry creeping up on him. "Nigga, you fool!" she shouted with a slur.

"Sherry, go 'head with the bullshit. You drunk," Tre replied, trying to avoid a confrontation.

"Oh, it's go 'head now, but it's not that when I'm sucking your dick, now is it?" Sherry snapped, drawing attention to herself with her hands on her hips.

"Sherry, get the fuck out of here with that bullshit! You ain't my broad!" Tre barked, clearly upset.

"Nigga, fuck you!" Sherry shouted before spitting in his face.

Before Tre could react, Shelly Mack came from out of nowhere, yanking Sherry by the hair.

"Bitch! you crazy! You done spit on the wrong nigga!" Shelly Mack shouted, landing a punch to her face. Sherry collapsed to the ground hard. Jumping back to her feet, Sherry charged Shelly Mack like an outraged bull. Being though Shelly Mack was raised by her male cousins, she side-stepped Sherry like a pro, connecting a two-piece combo. Sherry went tumbling down again; this time, Shelly Mack was digging in her ass like a thong, throwing blows after blows.

"Oh, shit. She's fucking her up," a bystander commented.

"Gurl, you ain't lying. That couldn't have been me," another one chimed in.

Pissed like hell, but feeling sorry for her at the same time, Tre pulled Shelly Mack up off of her.

"I told you to go 'head, Sherry. Now look at you. You made a fool of yo'self," Tre said, still holding Shelly Mack back.

Getting up, Sherry looked like she'd been in a boxing fight and had lost all twelve rounds. "Fuck you, nigga! You will get yours!" she yelled, limping away.

Let me go, Tre! I'ma beat that bitch ass again!" Shelly Mack yelled.

"Chill out, baby Ali. She got the message," Tre said, bum-rushing through the crowd. Tre made sure Shelly Mack got to her car okay.

"You need to go, cuz. You know someone done called the police by now. And don't trip on that, I'll handle Sherry's ass," Tre assured her.

"Ok, cousin, I'm out. But you know I'll beat that bitch ass if she comes off wrong out o' her mouth again," Shelly Mack replied, backing out and pulling off.

Walking back to his Range Rover, Tre's cell phone went off. Thinking it was Sherry's crazy ass, he looked at the screen. Seeing it was Tommy, he answered, "What's good, homie?"

"Damn son, why little cuz beat her ass like that?"

"Man, Sherry was on some bullshit," Tre replied.

"Well, me and Nice is on our way to the Gold Club. We heard they got some down south hotties up in there tonight."

"Man, y'all go 'head. I think I had enough excitement for one night," Tre replied.

"Say no more, son. I will get up with you tomorrow about that other thing too. Everything is everything," said Tommy before hanging up.

CHAPTER 15: PEACHES AND CREAM

As Tommy and Nice approached the front entrance of the Gold Club, the two sensed the jealousy of the haters anxiously waiting for admittance. Confident and bold as if they owned the place, they strolled right up to the six-foot-three, two hundred and sixty pounds bouncer.

"What's good, Troy?" Nice said.

"You know, women and money. We got some new girls for y'all tonight from down south; they some beauties too. I think y'all will like what you see," said Troy.

"That's why we're here," Nice replied.

The Gold Club was known as Wilmington's number one strip joint in the city. It was not only a strip joint but a gentlemen's club as well. Some of the sexiest chicks in the tri-state area worked there. While passing the bouncer a couple of dollars for cutting the line, you could see and hear all the sighs from angry niggas waiting in line.

"Hey, y'all. If looks could kill, y'all would be some dead muthafuckers," Troy joked.

"Niggas know what it is," Tommy shouted back as they entered the club.

The club was packed with ballers and wannabe ballers from all over the New Castle County. As the two made their way towards the bar, all eyes were on them. They had a couple of dollars before, but now it showed that they had big money.

"Hey, sexy, let me get two bottles of Rosé and two double shots of Hennessey," Nice shouted over Plies song 'Hypnotize.' From all the sexy women present, they definitely had eyes glued to them. After receiving their drinks, the two made their way over to the table. Tommy's chain was the center of attraction; the attention from all the gawking eyes was proving it.

"Damn, son, this shit is live as fuck!" Tommy shouted as he eyed Jaguar. Jaguar was Gold Club's main attraction, but tonight, they laid it out with some of down south finest from Magic City's strip club. Nice was eyeing one of them, loving every bit of it.

"Damn, Peaches, it's some ballers up in here," said Cream.

"These cats from Delaware is doing it up real big, huh?"

"Sure is," Peaches replied, looking over at Tommy and Nice. "Look at them two fine ass niggas. Especially the big one. His chain definitely hangs low."

"Well, let's go over there and get some of that money bitch!" Cream said.

As Peaches and Cream were approaching them, Nice and Tommy were being occupied by another stripper. She was short and thick as hell; double jointed and bowlegged with hot pink in her hair, and wore a red, white, and blue G-string with stars covering her nipples.

"You two trying to have some fun?" the stripper asked, dancing slowly and seductively.

"Yo, what type of fun you talking, shawdy?" Tommy replied.

"The both of you at the same time," the stripper shot back, sucking on her index finger and pointing at them with the other.

"How much you talking?" Nice inquired.

"One thousand for the both of you," she replied.

Nice looked at Tommy. Both burst out laughing.

"Is there something funny?" she asked, now standing still with both hands on her hips.

"Yeah, if you think you're getting that much," Nice replied, still laughing.

"You got to pay the way you weigh for this. But I guess this is the broke section," she said, before storming off.

"Well, call us when it's on sale," Nice yelled back. He and Tommy started laughing again.

Peaches and Cream witnessed the whole scene that just took place. At first they were skeptical about approaching them. But they were ten times better than the other chick.

"Are y'all treating all the women like that?" Peaches questioned.

Focusing their attention on the two beauties in front of them, Tommy and Nice were truly amazed. Cream was standing there looking like a younger version of Nia Long with her short hair style and caramel complexion. She was 5' 8", 160 pounds, with a small waist, but her ass cheeks and thighs were a show-stopper. Peaches on the other hand was looking like Stacey Dash with a Trina ass.

Cream leaned over and whispered in Peaches' ear.

"Bitch, look at that nigga's chain. That's Fat Cat's shit. I know that chain and charm from anywhere," Cream mumbled.

"Oh, gurl, you right," Peaches replied, focusing her attention on the chain that hung around Tommy's thick neck.

"What y'all two whispering about?" Nice barked, grabbing his crotch. "You know that's not polite."

"We're talking about how we're going to put it on y'all," Peaches replied, making her ass cheeks clap right where she stood.

"Gurl, I'll be right back," Cream said before walking off towards the dressing room. Inside the dressing room, Cream grabbed her cell phone from her bag and walked into the bathroom stall. Once the coast was clear, she dialed her brother.

*****

Trap was enjoying some super head when his cell phone started going off, picking up the cell he answers, "Whas'up, sis?"

"You not going to believe this shit," Cream replied in a low tone.

"Sssss, damn! Believe what, sis?" he asked,

"Some nigga from up Delaware is rockin' Fat Cat's chain," Cream informed him.

"What!!! Are you sure?" Trap replied, jumping up. The female sucking his manhood didn't stop sucking away.

"Nigga, you know I know what his chain looks like. He had it on the night you was supposed to handle that situation. It's one-of-a-kind, but the question is why do this nigga way up here have it hanging around his neck and how?" Cream said, peeking out of the bathroom stall to make sure no one was listening.

"Got damn, gurl!" he moaned.

"Trap, I know you ain't getting yo dick sucked while talking to me."

"Well, you did catch me at a bad time."

"Come on now. I'm serious, bro."

"Alright, alright. Stay on that nigga. Let me hit up Slow Juice. But whatever you do, don't let him out of your sight," Trap re-plied, at the point of exploding. After hanging up, Trap dialed Slow Juice.

"What's up, shawdy?" Slow Juice answered.

"Shit, big homie, you're not going to believe this."

"What's happening, nigga? Talk to me," Slow Juice replied.

"Sis just hit me and said that some nigga from up Delaware is rockin' that nigga Fat Cat's chain. That night that shit went down, he had that same chain on," Trap said.

"Word, if that's the case, she need to stay on that, you feel me, 'cause if that nigga got the chain, he must have that bread, you feel me."

"That's what I was thinking, big homie," Trap said.

"When Cream get back at you, you need to go and handle that, you feel me," Slow Juice ordered and hung up. Slow Juice was from Atlanta, Georgia, home of the peach trees. He recently came home from doing a fed bid. From bank robberies to local hood capers, Slow Juice did it all. Now back in his habitat, he was thirsty to get his feet wet again.

Niggas is trippin' if they think a muthafucka is going to come in my city and get away with some shit, you feel me, Slow Juice was thinking.

*****

Walking back towards the floor, Cream noticed Peaches handling her business. Nice and Tommy were making it rain.

"Can I get some of that money?" Cream said, strolling over to Nice.

"Sweetie, we've been waiting on you," replied Nice, placing twenty dollars into her strap.

"How about we get up out of here and really enjoy ourselves tonight?" Cream suggested, leaning in and licking the back of Nice's neck.

"Say no more," Nice replied, tapping Tommy to join him.

*****

A half an hour later, the group was at The Double Tree Hotel. Inside the suite, Peaches and Cream were in the bathroom getting prepared. At the same time, Nice and Tommy were on the couch rolling up some exotic weed. They were both lighting up when the girls exited the bathroom.

"Y'all smoke?" Tommy asked.

"We sure do," Peaches replied, walking towards Tommy in a voluptuous way. With him in front of her, she saddled his lap.

"Y'all wouldn't by any chance have some e-pills, would you?" Cream asked, eyeing Nice.

"And you know it," Nice replied, exposing a clear sandwich bag of e-pills of all sorts. Standing up, Nice grabbed a glass and filled it up with cold water.

"Oh no, sweetie, I don't take mine's like that," Cream said.

"Well, how do you take it then?" Nice asked, confused.

"Like this," Cream replied, turning around and spreading her ass cheeks.

Noticing a tattoo that read 'Enter at Your Own Risk' on her lower back, Nice didn't hesitate to place the ecstasy pill into her rectum with his thumb.

"Yo son, give me one," Tommy said, anxious to place one into Peaches' rectum as well.

"No, no, big boy, I take mine's like this," Peaches instructed, scooting backwards and spreading her pussy lips.

Tommy stuck the light blue pill deep into her pussy while playing with her now-swollen clitoris.

Opening her legs even wider, Peaches was enjoying the finger action.

Within fifteen minutes, it was on and poppin'. Peaches and Cream were having a dick-sucking marathon, sending Tommy and Nice both into a frenzy. They experienced hours of a non-stop sex session and the way Cream was poppin that pussy had Nice's mind twisted up.

That was truly a night to remember, and that was part of the plan; Peaches and Cream made sure of that....

CHAPTER 16: I WANT TO KNOW THE REAL YOU

"Son, let me tell you about last night," Tommy said to Tre as they sat in the church's parking lot on 22nd and Bowers Street. "Me and Nice freaked the fuck out of these two bitches from The Gold Club, yo. Word is bond, them bitches was some pill poppin' animals."

"I'm glad y'all had some fun last night, 'cause I didn't. That bitch Sherry wouldn't stop calling my cell phone. I could've sworn I'd seen her creeping past my crib. The way cuz beat her ass, I kinda felt sorry for her. But after the way she been acting, this bitch is really crazy. I could've sworn I heard that bitch at my front door too," Tre replied.

"Word, son, you got yourself a real live ass fatal attraction shit going on with you, kid," Tommy laughed.

"Ha, ha, ha. So what's up with yo peoples. Was everything good?"

"No doubt, son. Everything was everything, but the only problem is that he was only able to cover ten kilos," Tommy informed him.

"Ten keys! What the fuck! How we going to split that? I need that my damn self," Tre replied heatedly.

"I know, yo. That's why I'm only taking three keys, and you take the rest. Mar making like four thousand off each ounce out in New Castle, so three should hold him off until things get back right," Tommy said.

"Good looking, 'cause I know for a fact C-low going to knock off most of it," Tre replied.

"That's one money-getting muthafucka right there, son," stated Tommy, passing Tre the bag filled with work.

"Damn, Tommy, you got all of that exotic weed up in this muthafucka, don't you?" Tre asked, smelling the sweet odor in the air.

"Yeah, that's twenty pounds of that dumb shit for Nice."

"Yeah, I will definitely be hitting that nigga up for some of that," Tre assured him, giving Tommy some hand daps before getting out of the car and heading towards his truck. Once inside the truck, Tre hit C-low on the cell phone. He had to make sure he got straight before driving down to Miami. He couldn't wait to see Casina's face again.

*****

The sun was shining and the temperature was already in the low 90s at high noon. Tre was now back in Miami and when you saw Casina, you saw Tre. He couldn't take his mind off of her. She was like a goddess, the type of female that a man could only dream of. Tre was just hoping and praying that he wasn't dreaming.

In such a short period of time, Tre became large in the drug game. Not like Boston George type of money, but he was definitely a major player in the city of Wilmington. What normally takes some hustlers years to do, he was able to accomplish in months. Thanks to C-low 's help, of course, Tre's name was being mentioned in every barbershop and beauty salon in the city.

Tre always could dress his ass off, but now it was even more flamboyant. Dressed in his Gucci tank-top with a pair of white Gucci linen shorts and Gucci sneakers, Tre gazed intently at Casina sitting in his passenger seat through his new Gucci frames. Removing his aviator frames, he studied her with admiration.

"What you lookin' at?" she asked, eyeing him suspiciously.

"You, of course," Tre replied, looking deep into her eyes.

"I know you're looking at me, smarty. But why are you looking at me like that?" she asked giving him the same stare.

"'Cause, sweetie, I want to know you. The real you."

Feeling awkward, Casina threw up a defensive wall. "What do you mean, 'the real me'?" she asked with a confused look.

"Slow down, baby. I just wanted to know your story. Like where you live and how come we haven't been there yet? And why I never hear you talking about your family or anybody?"

Not prepared for that question, Casina was lost in her own thoughts when her eyes filled with tears. She really hadn't talked about her mother or father in years. That was a chapter in her life she didn't want to bring back up. All those emotions and frustration were building up and seemed to start surfacing all at once. Looking out of the passenger side window, Casina started telling him the story of her family. After she finished, more tears flooded down her face. Feeling embarrassed, she hid her face.

"It's cool, sweetie. You can cry. It's better out than in," Tre assured her, reaching his arm around her shoulders and pulling her closer to him.

It felt like the world had been lifted up off of her shoulders; for once in her life, Casina felt that love. It was the same love she once felt when her parents were alive.

"I just really need to get out of that house with my brothers. Too many bad memories," she said in between sobs. "I feel trapped."

Still rubbing her shoulders, Tre looked down at her.

"Don't worry, sexy. I got you now," he consoled her, pulling off and heading back towards the hotel.

*****

The next morning, Tre was still feeling aggrieved for Casina's past. The story she unfolded was still fresh on his mind. Wanting to do something nice, Tre spent the entire morning sightseeing and shopping. It was only one o' clock in the afternoon and he already spent well over eight thousand dollars. But he didn't care; money was his last name. And, seeing the smiles on Casina's face was well worth it.

Driving down Collins Ave., Tre noticed a sign that read 'Condos and Penthouses for sale, overlooking South Florida's most glorious Beach front' one mile ahead. As they pulled up to the Akoya, Casina eyed him suspiciously.

"Why are we here?"

"I thought we could look at some condos," he replied, smiling and licking his lips, trying his best to do LL Cool J impression.

Seconds later, Casina's door opened up. Caught off guard, she jumped. Tre reacted by reaching for his gun that was tucked away in his hidden compartment. Noticing it was only the attendant from valet parking, Tre calmed down. Allowing the valet attendant to do his job, Tre and Casina got out of the car and hurried through the front entrance.

On the inside, Casina was truly amazed. Everything was exotic and luxurious. As Tre stood over by the counter, Casina was soaking up the scenery. Within minutes, Tre and Casina were greeted by a beautiful Spanish host.

"Hello, my name is Selena. And I will be giving you two a tour of our beautiful building as well as the outside amenities," she informed them, eyeing Tre.

"We'll appreciate it," Casina replied, feeling kind of disrespected.

"Ok, follow me this way, please," Selena directed them, adding an extra bounce into her walk.

"You'll see that here at the Akoya, we offer high-ended one, two, and three-bedroom condos. We also have exclusive Penthouses. Every home boasts top-of-the-line features and designer finishes. From European style kitchens with name brand stainless steel appliances and granite countertops to marble master bathrooms with luxurious whirlpool tubs. Here, homeowners enjoy nothing but the best of the best at all times," she said, turning back to face them.

"Impressive," Tre remarked.

"Thank you, Mr. Money. Now if you look to the left, you'll see an on-site, state-of-the-art fitness center. And from the look of it, I see someone loves working out," she stated, checking out Tre's physique.

This bitch has the nerve, but I'ma keep my cool though before I catch a case, Casina thought while grabbing a hold of Tre's arm.

Selena continued, "As you can see, you have a beautiful beachfront right here. But if you want to go to South Beach, it's only minutes away. To enjoy all of this, the price ranges from 340 thousand to 1.1 million. But with a name like yours, Mr. Money, I see that won't be a problem," she remarked, making eye contact with Tre once again. She didn't care that Casina was present. She'd seen something that she liked and wanted it.

"Ok, Ho-lena, I mean Selena. We'll be in touch," Casina butted in, not feeling this bitch at all. Pulling Tre down the hall, Casina added an extra bounce to her walk to show Selena how it was supposed to be done.

CHAPTER 17: THERE'S ALWAYS SOMEONE WATCHING

Lyrics of Rick Ross' new hit blared in the car, loud enough to wake up the dead as C-low maneuvered down Fourth Street. Tre was back in town and C-low was on his way to meet up with him. The profit from the last bricks Tre had given him was tucked away in an orange-and-white Nike bag, under the passenger side seat.

Glancing through his rearview mirror, C-low observed a Crown Victoria. It was the same Crown Victoria he thought he had seen on Second Street earlier. He made a quick left onto Walnut Street and the Crown Victoria followed. C-low became immediately suspicious. He didn't know who was following him, but he sure as hell wanted to find out. Picking up his cell phone, he dialed Tre.

"What's good, C-low?" I'm waiting on you," answered Tre after the third ring.

"Shit, looks like I have a little situation here," C-low replied, glancing up at his rearview mirror.

"What you mean?"

"I think I'm being followed... nah, fuck that. I know I'm being followed," C-low clarified.

"You think it's the po-po or some stick-up boys?"

"Man, I'm not sure. They're driving in a Crown Victoria. It could be either one of them," replied C-low, grabbing his 9mm glock and placing in on his lap.

"Where you at now?"

"Coming down 17th street," C-low replied, keeping his eyes on the Victoria.

"Cool. I'm about to call Nice so we can find out who your little stalker is."

"So you still want me to come your way?"

"Yeah, ain't nothing change. Just meet me at Battlefield."

Anxious to find out who was tailing him, C-low followed Tre's instructions to a 'T.' Pulling up to Battlefield Park, he noticed Tre flicking his car's lights. C-low checked his rearview mirror one more time and tucked his glock before exiting the vehicle.

From afar, Detective Smith and Bush sat patiently, observing their prey.

"I told you, I would keep my end of the bargain," said Bush.

"We don't know shit yet," Smith replied, grabbing his binoculars. Focusing in on his mark, he was shocked to see Tre's face.

"Sooo, he's the man behind all of this," he thought to himself. Smith knew of Tre and his crew but they were never a factor before...until now. Pleased with what he saw, Smith pulled off.

Despite all of his police training, not once did he check his rearview mirror. 'Cause if he did, he would have noticed the green Dodge Charger following him. Minutes later, pulling back into a parking lot off of Maryland Avenue, Smith and

Bush emerged from the Crown Victoria. Neither one of them expected their pictures to be taken as Nice sat in the distance and zoomed in.

"Perfect shots," Nice said to himself, pulling off.

Fifteen minutes later, Nice pulled back up to Battlefield Park. He spotted Tre and C-low on the benches, smoking. Exiting his vehicle, he approached them.

"What you find out, homie?" Tre asked Nice, passing the blunt filled with Kush to C-low. Nice passed the camera to Tre. As Tre scanned through the pictures, he noticed Detective Smith and a young boy. The young boy's face looked familiar, but he couldn't put his finger on who he was. C-low looked at the pictures and his face instantly twisted into rage.

"What the fuck! He's with a cop! His ass is dead!"

"Wait a minute. You know him?" asked Tre, pointing at the picture.

"Yeah. I thought I knew him," replied C-low, as thoughts of vengeance in his head.

"Damn!" Tre snapped.

"You want me to handle this?" offered Nice.

"Nah, this my mess. Best believe I'm going to handle this one," C-low assured them.

"Well, you do that. I'm going to think of something for our little cop friend," Tre replied. After smoking a few more blunts, they finished their business and went on their separate ways.

*****

Three days passed since C-low saw Bush's picture. C-low and his crew met up in an abandoned house on Pleasant Street.

All eyes were on C-low as he paced back and forth. His crew waited patiently for him to say something.

"I called this emergency meeting for a reason. Every time something is going good, there's always a weak link somewhere trying to fuck it up," said C-low, stopping to look at the faces of his crew.

"One of you are betraying this crew. And I know which one of you it is," he barked. "I just want to see if you're man enough to stand up!"

The group of young goons all scanned each other, wondering who was the weakling. Off in the corner sat Bush, nervous as hell. He wondered if he had been exposed. As C-low paced through the room, he passed through each crew member. He stopped dead in his tracks when he approached Bush. Looking Bush in his eyes, C-low had seen the weakness. Bush knew he had been exposed.

"You pussy ass nigga!" C-low shouted.

"Wait, C-low, I can explain," pleaded Bush.

"WHACK! WHACK! WHACK!" was all that could be heard as C-low smacked Bush. "Explain what, little nigga? That you're a bitch made ass nigga?" he barked.

Holding his face, all Bush could do was look up at C-low with pleading eyes.

"I know you didn't think you was gonna cross me and get away with it? I trusted yo bitch ass! You were supposed to be my little homie," C-low said, pulling out a black snug nose .38 revolver. "I guess I was wrong, but like they say, never bite the hand that feeds you."

Bush's life flashed before him and as soon as he realized where he went wrong at, it ended: C-low 's six bullets were piercing his body.

C-low turned around to face the remainder of his crew, as if he was a teacher and a class was in session. "Is there anybody else that's talking to the fucking police? 'Cause if so, the same thing that just happened to him will happen to you," he said, reloading his weapon. "Nothing happens in these streets without me finding out about it. Let this be a lesson learned. You cross me, you will meet your maker! Now clean this shit up!" he ordered, turning away. His crew began cleaning up the bloody mess.

*****

The weather was breaking and fall was nearing, with the temperature dropping to the mid sixties. Hopping into Nice's truck was Cream, wearing a pink, white, and red-fitted Ed Hardy hooded jacket with skin tight jeans to match. Nice was enjoying every bit of her; Cream was beginning to have an effect on him. Lately, he'd caught himself doing things he thought he would never do. He was showering her with all sorts of gifts, spending quality time with her. His motto was 'Fuck 'em and Duck 'em.' But with Cream, it was different. It was as if they had some sort of bond, or so he thought.

"So where we going, with yo handsome self?" she asked, popping her gum.

"I thought we could go catch that new flick 'Hood Rich.' I heard that shit is funny as hell," he replied.

"It doesn't matter, as long as I'm with you, boo," she replied, pumping him up.

Just as Nice was pulling off, his Boost Mobile phone chirped. Seeing that it was his young boy, he turned the speaker off before answering it.

"What's good, little homie?"

"Shit, big homie, we getting low, low, and it's jumping," the young boy replied.

"Damn," Nice said, looking over at Cream.

"What's the matter, baby," she said.

"I have to handle something real quick."

"Okay," she replied, not seeing what the fuss was all about.

"I have to drop you back off so that I can go handle it."

"Baby, I thought we were going to watch the movie," she whined.

"We are, but let me handle this first. And I'll be right back."

"Why can't I come? I promise you won't even know I was there," she said. Reaching over, she unbuttoned his pants, removing her gum.

Nice turned to his Mobile. It chirped.

"Give me twenty to thirty minutes and I'll be through," said Nice.

"OK, big homie," the young boy replied.

Nice knew he should have just dropped Cream off first, but she was giving him one of his best blow jobs he had ever experienced. That alone was making it hard for him to think. Nice continued on driving with a new destination: the stash house. Ten minutes later, Nice pulled up to the stash house. Still sucking away, Cream popped her head up.

"Wait here," Nice ordered as he fixed his pants and hopped out of the truck, heading towards the house.

Scanning her surroundings, Cream made a mental note of the area and the house Nice went into.

Soon, Nice emerged with a bag in his hand. Back in the truck, Nice threw the bag in the back seat. Smelling the strong marijuana in the air, Cream's suspicion was answered.

"Bingo," she thought as they pulled off.

CHAPTER 18: LAST I CHECKED, I WAS GROWN

Ricky noticed a change in his sister. He'd been hearing a lot of things about her around the city. It was now beginning to get under his skin. He could hear her coming from the kitchen.

"Casina, come here."

"What you want?" she sighed.

"What am I hearing about you parading around the city with an out-of-towner?"

"What?" she shot at him with an attitude. "Last time I checked I was grown." She hated the fact that people always ran back telling her brothers her business.

"Your grown ass never stops to think that this nigga might be using you to get at me and Rayman?" Ricky shot back. At that point, Rayman came walking through the door.

"So, I'm not supposed to have a life 'cause of the lifestyle y'all choose to live?" Casina began yelling, pissed as hell. "That's not fair, and I doubt my friend needs y'all money, 'cause he got his own!"

"Y'all two need to chill with that. Now what's going on?" Rayman questioned.

113

"No! She's being stupid about the situation. She don't understand how the game go. They get closer to someone that we love just so that they can get at us," said Ricky.

"I hate you! If daddy was alive I wouldn't be going through this!" Casina yelled as she stormed up towards her room. Her words penetrated Ricky like a sharp object. He didn't mean for it to get out of hand.

"Now, was that called for? She's not little no more, you know. Everybody she meets is not out to get us, Ricky."

"I guess I'm still pissed about the Fat Cat shit."

"Bro, that's nothing," Rayman replied.

"I'm not talking about the money. We don't even know who else was involved. That means it could be anybody. That pussy ass nigga Magic was tougher than I expected. He went to the grave with his info," Ricky told him.

"Man, forget all that. You need to take yo ass upstairs and talk to sis. You know we're the only family we got," Rayman replied.

When Ricky got to her room, he noticed the room was empty and clothes were scattered everywhere. Hearing noise out front, Ricky went to the window and saw Casina pulling off. *Women*, thought Ricky, shaking his head as he headed back downstairs.

******

"Chica, I can't stand Ricky. He acts like he's my father. Last I saw, my father was dead!"
Casina sobbed as tears poured down her cheeks.

"I know, I know. It's going to be okay," Lolita assured her, giving her a hug. "You can stay here for the weekend until you get yourself together. And, it's my birthday this weekend, bitch. You know we're going to do it up like divas," Lolita told her, giving her a hug.

At that moment, Casina's phone began to ring. Hearing the lyrics of 'Rock Boys' by Jay-Z, Casina became excited.

"Hello," Casina answered, clearing her throat.

"What's the matter, sweetie?" Tre replied, sensing something was wrong.

"The usual, arguing with my stupid ass brother."

"It sounds like my baby needs a weekend getaway."

"I can't, baby. I'm supposed to spend the weekend with Lolita...it's her birthday weekend."

"That's even better. The both of y'all can come," Tre proposed.

"Oh, both of us can come?" she said, looking at Lolita for approval. Lolita gave her thumbs-up.

"I guess we can do that," said Casina.

"Well, good. That's what I wanted to hear. Two first class tickets will be waiting for the two of you," he assured her.

"I hope he has someone for me? 'Cause I'm not trying to be the third wheel," Lolita said, loud enough for Tre to hear.

Hearing her in the background, Tre responded, "Tell her not to sweat it. I'll have everything under control."

After hanging up, Casina and Lolita got their drinks on. Listening to Mary J. Blige's new CD, they tried to get their things together for the weekend.

"Gurl, we have to go shopping," said Lolita, assisting Casina with packing her stuff.

"Gurl, we just went shopping," Casina reminded her.

"I know, but the weather is cooler up north."

"Oh shit. Chica, you right," Casina said. Grabbing her cellphone, she checked the weather in Wilmington, Delaware, for the weekend. "Damn, Chica. We definitely have to go shopping, gurl."

"Well, bitch, what we waiting for?" Lolita replied, jumping up and grabbing her car keys.

Five and a half hours later, Casina and Lolita were back at Lolita's apartment packing and getting their drink on. Both of them were wondering what the weekend would look like. One thing they did know was that they were going to look good doing it.

*****

Remembering Casina telling him that Lolita was a Spanish chick, Tre had the perfect person in mind. He picked up his cell phone and dialed. It began to ring.

"What's good?" a voice answered.

"What's poppin'?" Tre asked.

"Shit, chillin'" came the response.

"You trying to have a little fun this weekend?"

"Hell yeah. A nigga always trying to have some fun."

"Well, good. My female friend is bringing her girl up with her. It's her girl's birthday. I told her we would show her a good time," Tre told the person. After hanging up, Tre sat back and began planning for the upcoming festivities.

*****

The next morning, Detective Smith was enjoying his blueberry donuts and coffee when a female voice came blaring over the CB Radio. "All units, respond to a possible homicide on Second and Harrison Street."

"Damn," Smith thought as he pulled out of Dunkin' Donuts' parking lot with his blue and red lights flashing, heading towards the west side of the city.

Pulling up, Smith saw the yellow tape. Approaching the crime scene, he recognized the rookie cop kneeling down by the body bag.

"What do we have here?" Detective Smith asked, still sipping his coffee.

"We haven't identified the body yet, but we believe he's between the ages of sixteen to eighteen. Multiple gunshot wounds to the torso. And we discovered his tongue has been removed," the rookie cop informed him, unzipping the bag and exposing the body.

When Detective Smith laid eyes on the corpse, he damn near choked on his coffee.

"Sir, is everything okay?" the rookie cop asked.

"Yes, you can zip it back up," said Detective Smith.

Seeing Bush's lifeless body like that did something to him. He knew it was his fault that Bush was now another victim of the streets.

Loud music startled Detective Smith from behind and he turned to see C-low's vehicle creeping by the crime scene. Rolling down his window, C-low let his presence be felt as he flashed a sinister smile at the detective.

At the point of exploding, Detective Smith held back his anger and headed towards the vehicle.

"I've got to get this bastard," he vowed.

CHAPTER 19: WHERE THE BALLERS BALL AND THE PLAYERS PLAY

"Gurl, I'm sure glad we went shopping," Lolita said, zipping her up jacket.

"Who you telling?" Casina replied, crossing her arms to keep warm.

Walking out of Philadelphia International Airport was like walking into a room with air conditioning on blast. The weather was a major difference to the weather in Miami. Reaching for her cell, Casina noticed Tre and another male walking up towards their direction, pulling luggage behind them. Walking right up to her, Tre gave her a hug and a kiss.

"Baby, why do you have luggage? Am I missing something?"

"We will be if we don't hurry up. I'll explain on the way," Tre assured her.

"Oh, I'm rude. This is my best friend Lolita," Casina introduced.

"How you doing birthday girl?" Tre asked.

"Fine, so you're the one I've been hearing so much about," Lolita replied, eyeing his friend.

Catching her stare, Tre introduced his friend. "This is my homie, C-low."

"How y'all doing?" C-low said, staring Lolita up and down.

"We doing fine," Lolita replied, giving him a stare of her own.

"You sure are," teased C-low.

"I don't mean to break up y'all thing, but we do have a flight to catch," Tre said.

"Baby, so where we going?" Casina asked with a puzzled look.

"Vegas, baby, where the ballers ball and the players play," Tre replied, leading the way towards the plane.

Once on the plane, Casina and Tre were seated together while C-low and Lolita sat across from them, engaged in a deep conversation. A few hours later, the group landed. As soon as they exited the plane and hit the inside of the Vegas airport, Tre noticed slot machines everywhere. *Damn, they don't be bullshitting* he thought.

Outside, they were hypnotized by the atmosphere and the luminous lights. Night fell, but not that anyone could tell. Night was considered day for the people who partied in Sin City. Las Vegas was the place to be; this is where Bugsy Seigel laid down the law and the Rat Pack laid down the style. It was truly the city that never slept. It was a 24 hours, 7 days a week place where only the money was real. If the crowds in the casinos are too big, the four-mile stretch of Las Vegas Blvd., known to many as the 'Strip', was the world capital of gleaming and pleasurable palaces. There were also cheap, all-you-can-eat buffets and quick-hitch wedding chapels. Furthermore, all the exotic women parading around would drive any man crazy. But that wouldn't bother Tre or C-low; they had two of the most attractive females out of Miami.

Dressed in Christian Dior jackets with the matching boots and frames, Casina and Lolita were kind of upset. They weren't prepared for this weather; it was just as hot in Vegas as it was back home in Miami. Seeing the expression on her face, Tre knew something was bothering her. "What's the matter, sweetie?" he asked, flagging down a taxi cab.

I wished you would have told me before we went shopping," she pouted. "I was thinking we was going to be in cooler weather."

"Don't trip. I told y'all, we got everything under control."

Twenty-five minutes later, they were standing inside the Wynn Hotel lobby. Tre booked a Presidential Suite for the weekend. Once upstairs and inside the Presidential Suite, their jaws dropped. It looked more like an apartment than a hotel suite. Everything was top-of-the-line. A spacious Jacuzzi smacked dab in the middle of the room. It also had two Master Suite bedrooms, a pull-out couch, and mini bars filled with top shelf liquor.

Spotting the liquor bottles, C-low ambled over to the mini bar, "Now this is what I'm talking about," he said, holding up a bottle of Hennessy XO.

"Now you talking my language," Lolita followed suit.

Scanning the mini bar, Tre didn't see what he was looking for. Walking towards the hotel phone, he called room service.

"Can I have six bottles of Rosé delivered to my suite, please?" Tre asked.

"Yes sir, will that be all?" the female replied.

"Yes, for now," Tre said. Hanging up, Tre walked over to his top-of-the-line suitcase. Once it was opened, he pulled the hidden compartment. Inside was one hundred and fifty thousand dollars in cash. Removing a small amount, he turned towards Casina.

"Here, sweetie, I heard they have the top designers here," he said, passing her twenty thousand dollars.

"Thank you, babes," she replied, giving him a kiss.

"You're welcome. If y'all need more, let me know. And get something nice for tomorrow night. We have big plans for you and the birthday girl," Tre told her.

With that said, Casina and Lolita went off to do what they did best - shop.

After their short shopping spree, the duo headed back to the hotel suite. As soon as they waltzed in, the smell of marijuana and a cloud of smoke greeted them.

"I didn't know you smoked?" said Casina questioningly, as they approached them on the couch.

"Yeah, I smoke here and there," replied Tre. "I hope it's not a problem?"

"No, it's cool," she assured him.

"I'll take it that y'all don't smoke?" asked C-low.

"I surely do," said Lolita, sitting right next to him.

Sensing that Casina probably felt left out, Tre passed the blunt back to C-low and walked to her.

"So, baby, what you get?" he asked, leaning over to rub her shoulders.

The touch of his hands sent chills down her spine.

"We grabbed a few things from a couple of stores," said Casina, stepping in closer. The smell of Issey Miyake on him was turning her on. Tre grabbed her lower back and pulled her even closer as he began kissing her passionately.

"Eww, y'all making me sick!" commented Lolita, pretending to throw up before inhaling the sweet bud.

"Yeah, cut all of that lovey-dovey shit out. We're here to do it up," C-low joked.

"Stop hating," laughed Casina before planting one more kiss on Tre.

An hour and a half later, they were all showered and dressed to impress. Tre was wearing the latest Tru Religion jeans with a V-neck Argyleculture t-shirt to match. The slip-on Mauri shoes he had complemented his outfit to the 'T.' C-low had on some Black Label jeans and the shirt to show off his slim frame along with a pair of hi-top Prada sneakers. Not to mention they both were draped in iced-out jewelry.

Looking as gorgeous as ever; Casina was styling in a pair of Prada skinny jeans, a strapless Prada shirt that showed off her flawless skin, and a pair of black peep-toe Prada heels. By her side, Lolita was killing them in her skin-tight Fendi dress with the platform sandals to match. They were ready for what Vegas had to offer and headed out of the suite.

Taking the elevator down seemed like a ride, as they were all anxious to get their gambling on.

"Baby, I've never gambled before. What do I do?" asked Casina.

"Well, sweetie, try playing the Roulette table," suggested Tre, passing her two thousand dollars in cash. "I've seen a lot of females playing there and at the slot machines too."

"And this is for you, birthday girl," C-low offered, handing Lolita two thousand dollars as well so she wouldn't feel left out. Exiting the elevator, they saw a site that seemed to be only for a gambler's eyes. With all the lights from the machines and the sounds of winners, they were ready to play.

Casina and Lolita headed over to the Roulette table while Tre and C-low ambled towards the Crap table. Tre and C-low both cashed in five thousand dollars for chips, waiting to see who was the hot roller before placing any bets.

Meanwhile, over at the Roulette table, Casina and Lolita were having a hard time.

"So, how do we play this game again?" Casina asked the older lady running the game.

"You bet on numbers. I will drop this ball into the revolving wheel and it will land on a number. Hopefully, that lucky number will be yours," the older lady explained.

"What numbers are you going to bet on?" Casina asked Lolita.

"Gurl, my birthday of course," Lolita responded, exchanging her money for chips.

Still undecided, Casina didn't know what numbers to pick.

"Which one pays the most?" she asked, scanning over the numbers on the table.

"Double zero," the older lady replied.

Not thinking, Casina placed two one-hundred dollar chips down on the double zero box.

"You sure you want to place that bet, young lady?" the older lady asked.

"You only live once, right?" replied Casina, smiling.

The older lady made sure all the players' bets were final before dropping the small shining ball into the spinning wheel.

"Click! Click! Click! Click!"

When the wheel came to a stop, Casina couldn't believe her eyes. It was on double zeros.

"We have a winner!" the older lady announced, passing Casina four chips.

"This is all I get?" Casina asked, looking at the chips with a puzzled look.

"Bitch, that's twenty thousand dollars!" Lolita yelled, pointing at the numbers on the chips.

Focused on the numbers engraved onto the chips, Casina's mouth dropped. Snatching the four chips and placing them into her Prada bag, Casina continued on gambling with the remainder chips. For the next hour, Casina was on a roll. She was now up to forty-two thousand dollars in chips. On the other hand, Lolita was losing like hell. But she didn't mind because she was having fun doing it.

Tre noticed the girls walking towards them, "Here, you need more chips?" he asked, reaching for his pile of chips.

"I was going to ask you the same question," Casina replied with a smile, showing off the pile of chips she had in her bag.

Tre couldn't believe what his eyes were seeing. "Damn, baby, you won all that?" Tre asked in shock.

"Well, what can I say? I was on a roll," she cockily replied.

"Hold the dice, shooter!" Tre said, pointing at the many numbers before them. "Baby, point to any number box."

Following her finger, Tre placed a thousand-dollar bet on the number she picked. He looked at the man holding the dice and nodded his head. With a few shakes of the hand, the man released the dice. When the two big red and white dice came to a stop, Tre couldn't believe it: Casina had just won him sixteen thousand dollars.

"Damn, baby, I should have had you over here twenty minutes ago," he smiled before giving her a kiss.

"If I would have known you would have kissed me like that, I would have been over here too," she replied, grabbing a hand full of his manhood where none could see.

An hour later, they were all in the club enjoying themselves. With bottles of Rosé on the table and mixed drinks in their hands, Casina and Lolita were tipsy and they knew it. Slipping away, C-low waltzed over towards the DJ booth and whispered something in his ear while passing him some money. Tre knew C-low was up to something when he came back smiling. Next thing you knew the DJ's voice came through the speakers.

"This next one is for a sexy lady by name of Lolita. C-low says 'Happy Birthday'."

When the spotlight shined on her, Lolita's mouth dropped. Then, 'In Da Club' by 50 Cent filled the air. At that point, Lolita jumped up and ran into C-low 's arms, giving him a hug and a kiss on his cheek.

"Thank you," she said, turning around to back her soft butt up on him. C-low couldn't have denied the feeling. The connection between them was there, above the fact that he was attracted to her as well. Casina and Tre laughed at the sight of their close friends. The group partied hard that night and enjoyed every minute of it.

The next evening, they all dined out at an exquisite restaurant with an amazing view of the entire Las Vegas strip. Topping the night off, Tre surprised them with tickets to see Floyd Mayweather fight. The seats were so up close that when Floyd Mayweather knocked down his opponent, blood got on C-low 's pants.

The next morning, Casina and Lolita both went to the spa to get pampered. After the spa the girls then spent a few hours sightseeing and shopping. The weekend ended fast and all the fun Casina was having had to come to an end because she had finals to take on Monday. Picking up her cell phone, she dialed Tre's phone. On the second ring, he answered,

"Hey, baby."

"Hey, babe. You know I have class tomorrow," she pouted.

"I already took care of it, sweetie. I switched y'all flights to go straight to Miami," he replied.

"Thank you baby, you're the best."

"The best deserves the best," he assured her before ending the call.

Back at McCarran International Airport, they all said their goodbyes. Lolita really enjoyed herself; this weekend would be a weekend she would never forget. To show her appreciation, she kissed C-low on lips while their tongues danced passionately.

"Eww, y'all making me sick!" Casina pretended to throw up, mocking Lolita. They all burst out laughing, going their separate ways to catch their flights back home.

CHAPTER 20: ADDICTION

Barricaded in her room, Sherry was taking it hard. Not being able to be around Tre had taken a toll on her. With her hair matted and smelling like she hadn't bathed in days, she sat there, hunched over the coffee table.

"Sniff! Sniff....! Sniff! Sniff!"

"Fuck 'em, they say white treat you right anyway," she was thinking, referring to the white powdery substance spread out in small lines before her. The love she once had for Tre was now replaced with revenge and anger. Sherry's new love was Mr. Cocaine. High and out of her mind, she paced back and forth in her bedroom talking to herself. Sherry had literally cut off all communication with everyone in her circle as she drowned in her misery. Her emotions took over and vengeance sat in her bloodstream. She avoided all incoming calls and answering the door was out of the question.

"BOOM! BOOM! BOOM! BOOM!" The sound of knocking startled her.

"Sherry, open up! I know you're in there 'cause your car is out front!" Nye yelled as she banged on the front door. "BOOM! BOOM! BOOM!"

Geeked out of her mind, Sherry peeked through the blinds down at Nye. Nye was one of her clients, her hair was a hot mess, and she was in a desperate need of a hairdo. Nye hadn't talked to Sherry in weeks and she didn't get her hair styled by just anyone.

"Fuck!" Nye screamed, jumping back in her car and pulling off.

Once the coast was clear, Sherry did a few more lines before heading out of the house with a vengeful mind.

*****

The weather was unpredictable, jumping from cold to warm. It was mid-October with the temperature in the high sixties. Parked on Claymont Street, Nice and Cream sat in their truck smoking exotic weed while watching a DVD. Laughing at Mike Epps 'Next Friday,' Nice didn't notice Tre pulling up behind him. Getting out and walking up to the window, Tre noticed Nice had company with him.

"This is how people get killed," Tre stated, startling Nice.

"Whass'up, my nig? I didn't see you pulling up," Nice replied, facing him.

"I see, and who's your friend?" Tre inquired.

"Oh, this sexy thing here? Her name is Cream," Nice informed him, stroking the back of her hair.

"How you doing, Cream? A' Nice, let me rap with you real quick."

"What's poppin'?" Nice asked, hopping out of the truck.

"Here, I took a pound of that piff from the spot. My peoples C-low needed it," Tre said, passing him forty-five hundred in cash.

"Come on now, that's C-low. He could have given me thirty-two for that shit," Nice told him, counting out thirteen hundred to give back to Tre so he could give it back to C-low.

"VRROOM! VRROOM! VRROOM!"

"Look at this nigga," Tre pointed out as Tommy came flying down the street in his Ducati 999R.

Flying past them, Tommy jumped the curb, heading back towards their direction.

"Now you know yo big ass is too big to be on that bike. Where you get it from, Pep Boys?" Nice joked.

"Ha, ha, ha, very funny," retorted Tommy, getting off the bike.

"Nah, I'm fucking with you, big homie. Let me ride it?"

"Nah, son, you be wildin' too much. You ain't about to fuck my shit up."

"Ain't nobody going to fuck yo shit up," Nice assured him, hopping on the bike.

Nice's truck door swung open.

"Ohh! Can you give me a ride?" Cream yelled, hopping out of the truck.

Her jeans were fitting her plumpness like a glove when she came within eyesight. She hopped on the back of the bike with her ass propped up and her arms wrapped around Nice's waist. Nice hit the front break while accelerating, causing the back tire to burn out before zooming off.

"Son! Don't crash my shit!" Tommy yelled out as Nice darted down Claymont Street.

"Shortie phat as shit," Tre stated.

"Yeah, that's the shortie I was telling you about. That night me and Nice freaked her and her girl off. I called the other shortie, I guess she ain't fucking with a nigga," Tommy said.

129

"Damn, what you didn't dick her down right?" Tre laughed.

"Son, I put the pipe game down real good. You just know a nigga like me don't be spending no extra time or money on these hoes," Tommy let it be known.

"And that right there is the reason why yo ass ain't got no broad by yo side now," Tre joked.

"Whatever, nigga."

"Oh shit! I almost forgot. I have a haircut appointment."

"Word?"

"Yeah, I got to go," Tre said, giving Tommy some hand daps.

"Alright, I'll holla at you," Tommy replied as he looked up and down the street for Nice.

Jumping back into his Range Rover, Tre pulled alongside Tommy. "You know that nigga probably on Market Street by now."

"I ain't trippin', 'cause I'm about to take his truck so I can see if I can bag me a new chick," he replied, hopping in Nice's truck.

"Y'all crazy," Tre yelled as he pulled off. He was now on his way to 'Cut Above the Rest.'

*****

Meanwhile, on the west side of Wilmington, the streets were flooded with people and luxury cars. Fiends were out, which meant there was money to be made. The middle of Second Street between Franklin and Harrison was heavily occupied. A circle of hustlers and bystanders surrounded a rap battle that was happening.

"A' yo, a' yo, a lot of dudes talk sideways out of their mouth, until the whole squad is inside of their house, duct tape silence you out, point to the safe I'm taking it out, next time tell your spouse to close her mouth. I'm like a mouse all about my cheese," the skinny light-skinned boy rhymed. Oohs and aaahs filled the air when he was done dropping his bars.

"You right, you do talk sideways out of your mouth, but see, I'll catch you right outside of your house, put that thing to your brain, sweet dreams, while the blood leaks outside of your mouth!" the short dark-skinned boy rapped back.

"Oh shit, you heard what he just said! He killed him," a bystander said.

The rap battle was interrupted by C-low wheeling up the block from Harrison to Franklin Street. He was on his new black, blue, and white Suzuki G SXR 1000. He was rocking a blue-and-white racing jacket with his name on the back to complement his new bike. A couple of young hustlers came running up to him.

"Man, C-low, dis shit is dope," one of them said.

"Come on now, you can get yourself one too, little homie," C-low assured him, checking his cell phone. He noticed Lolita was calling and pushed the talk button.

In the distance, Detective Smith sat in his car, filled with rage. Not being able to take anymore of C-low showing off, he darted from his parking spot like a bat out of hell. Seeing the Crown Vic approaching him at top speed, C-low told Lolita that he would call her right back. Spinning his bike around like a Ruff Ryder, C-low burned rubber, shooting up Second Street like a bullet. With the Crown Vic speeding behind him, C-low's young goons chanted, "Go C-low! Go!" Shooting through red lights like a daredevil, by the time C-low reached Union Street, the Crown Vic wasn't in sight. Making a left turn, C-low headed over to Camby Park. After parking in a secluded area, he dialed Lolita back to finish their conversation.

*****

Walking out of 'Cut Above the Rest,' Twain had Tre looking like a million bucks. Twain was the best barber in Delaware. He had awards from competing in hair shows up and down east coast to prove it.

As he walked towards his Range Rover, Tre noticed his tires were flat.

"What the fuck!" Tre yelled, scanning his surroundings.

In the distance, sitting inside her Acura Legend, Sherry watched as he circled his truck.

"You haven't seen nothing yet," she thought, before hitting another bag of cocaine and pulling off.

After circling around the block a few more times, Detective Smith was pissed. C-low had made a fool out of him and he didn't like it one bit.

Turning down Lancaster Avenue, he was on his way back to the station when he caught sight of Tre standing next to his truck with flat tires. Pulling over to the KFC parking lot, he waited to see where Tre would lead him.

Pissed like hell, Tre was grabbing his cell to dial Triple A Car Services.

CHAPTER 21: TIME FOR PAYBACK

Relaxing inside the house on 22nd and Pine Street, Murda Mike and Smooth were playing NBA Live on XBox 360 when Skippie came strolling in.

"Remember you told me to find out who killed your little brother and his homies?" Skippie said to him.

"Yeah, speak, nigga," Murda Mike replied, focusing his attention on Skippie.

"Well, I heard that the nigga Nice had something to do with it," Skippie stated.

"What! That nigga that be selling weed on Claymont Street?" Murda Mike barked.

"Yeah, that nigga rolls with Tommy and Tre," Skippie replied.

"I don't give a fuck who he rolls with. I want you and Smooth to find that nigga and handle that," Murda Mike ordered.

Recently finishing his ten-year bid on a manslaughter charge, Murda Mike knew of Tre and Tommy very well. He witnessed how they became real close after Tommy helped Tre fight them prisoners at Chapel Service. But Nice crossed the line by killing his little brother. Neither Tommy nor Tre could stop what he had in store for Nice.

"KNOCK! KNOCK! KNOCK!"

"Who in the fuck is it?" Skippie yelled, walking towards the door with his gun in hand.

"Y'all working?" a female voice responded from the other side of the door.

Opening up the door, she came strolling in. Nobody would have thought in a million years that she was high.

"What the fuck do you want, 'cause you sure don't look like you smoke crack," Skippie replied, peeking out the door before closing it. Still with his gun in hand, he sized her up and down.

"Yeah, shortie, we stopped selling weed two months ago since the big homie came home," Smooth added.

Murda Mike sat in silence as he stared at the female that stood before him.

"I'm looking for a fifty of powder," she said, feeling out of place.

"So you sniff, huh?" Murda Mike asked, exposing a Ziploc bag filled with powder. Seeing the cocaine, she immediately started craving for it. Seeing how desperate she looked, Murda Mike made a small line on the table for her.

"There you go, sweetie," he said, pointing to the line of coke.

Not having to be told twice, she was down on her knees snorting away. After hitting the line, her nerves calmed down and she was craving for more.

"So, how much can I get for fifty?" she asked, holding up a crisp fifty-dollar bill.

"How about you put that money away, and let me see how badly you really want to get high?" Murda Mike said, pulling out his manhood and sprinkling coke on it, not caring who was watching.

Since cocaine was what she wanted and Murda Mike was the man with it, she crawled over to him and snorted the coke off his dick before placing it deep into her mouth. The magic she was performing with her mouth was sending him into a frenzy. Wanting some of the action, Smooth and Skippie watched while grabbing at their crotches.

"What the fuck y'all standing there for? Go and find that nigga Nice and handle that nigga," Murda Mike ordered.
Hearing Nice's name, she popped her head up. Were her ears playing tricks on her?

"What the fuck did you stop for? Suck this dick," Murda Mike barked before sprinkling more coke on his manhood.
Placing her lips back around his shaft, Sherry sucked him into ecstasy.

*****

She watched as he climbed into the bed, his well-formed body had her insides doing somersaults.

"I want some of that sweet dick," said Cream seductively as she began to climb on top of him.

Nice was fascinated by her body, so it was only natural that when his fingers touched the juices dripping from her pulsating pussy, he instantly got hard as a rock. The veins were bulging out of his penis, and the blood was rushing to the tip like a waterfall. After placing a condom on, Cream straddled him like the pro she was.

"Ssss... damn, girl... this pussy feels good as shit," Nice moaned, pushing deeper into her insides.

"You like this pussy? You like the way it feel?" Cream asked as she began to pick up the pace. She was rocking back and forth.

"Oh, she's trying to get into a nigga's head," Nice thought as he palmed both ass cheeks, spreading them apart for more access.

Cream rotated her hips in a circular motion as if she was riding a bull. The sweet sounds of ass smacking and pussy popping were echoing throughout the hotel room.

"Ssss... ohhh... I can feel you all up in my stomach....ssss... fuck this pussy... damn... right... there," she moaned before biting down her lower lip.

The knocks at the door interrupted their sexual flow of things.

"Cream! Why the hell do you have the top latch on?" Peaches yelled through the crack of the hotel door.

"Ohh... Ssss... shiiitt!" Creamed moaned as she tried to get as many strokes in as possible before she had to go and let Peaches in.

Hopping up off his penis, she grabbed her white robe. "I promise I'll make this up to you," she said while heading towards the front room, leaving him with a stiff one.

As soon as she opened the door, Peaches let her have it.

"Damn, bitch, what was you doing?" she protested as she stormed past Cream. Before Cream could respond, Peaches' question was answered when she saw Nice waltzing from out the back room fixing his clothes. Seeing the look Peaches gave him, Nice walked right past her as if she didn't exist.

"I have som'em to handle. Are we still on for tomorrow?" he asked Cream.

"Yes," she replied, giving him a kiss and a hug.

After Nice was gone and out of sight, Peaches let her have it. "What you doing? I know you're not falling for this nigga. Don't forget why we're here," she snapped.

"Gurl, whatever," Cream replied, brushing her off.

"Oh, it's gurl whatever. We will just have to see what Slow Juice have to say about this," Peaches replied before storming off towards the back. "And I hope you change these sheets too, with yo nasty ass!" she yelled from the back room.

Cream was confused as different emotions boiled up inside of her. Was she falling for Nice? Had she fallen in love with the enemy? These were the questions running through her mind. Questions that she couldn't answer at this time....

CHAPTER 22: I SEE DEATH AROUND THE CORNER

The lyrics from 'What's Beef' by Notorious B.I.G. blasted through the speakers as the two thugs cruised the north side of Wilmington in search for their victim.

"I'ma fill this nigga up with so many holes when we catch up with him," Smooth stated, loading up the bullets with an old t-shirt to avoid his fingerprints showing up on the bullets.

"Nigga, you faking. Just load the bullets up and keep your eyes on a lookout for this nigga," Skippie snarled.

"Oh, shit! There goes that mothafucka right there," Smooth yelled, pointing at their prey.

"Pass me my pistols, this nigga is about to die," Skippie said, his tone violent.

Coming out of Kennied Fried on Market Street, Nice took notice of a black van with tinted windows creeping up behind him. Hearing the sliding door open from the van, he reacted by hitting the unlock button on his keypad while lunging into his truck. Two masked men opened fire on his truck.
"POP! POP! POP! POP! POP! POP! BAP! BAP! BAP! BAP! BAP!" was all you heard as the two masked men pumped rapid shots into the truck.

Across the street, at a gas station, people scattered like roaches trying to avoid the gunplay.

"Bitch! Fuck them Dutches and come on!" Shelly Mack yelled, ducking down under her car.

"Ohhh! Shelly, ain't that your cousin friend they shooting at?" Kris asked, remembering that truck from the park that day at the softball game.

Focusing her attention on the direction of the two gunmen, Shelly noticed that it was indeed Nice's truck they were shooting at. Snatching her .380 caliber gun from out of her Gucci bag, Shelly sprung into action. Running across the street, she opened fire on the two masked men.

"POP! POP! POP! POP! POP!"

Turning in the direction of the gunshots, the two thugs could hear police sirens approaching. They fired off a few more rounds at the female before jumping back into the van and skidding off. Rushing to Nice's aid, Shelly Mack noticed blood all over him.

"Stay still, help is on the way," she assured him.

*****

Outside the Emergency Room entrance, Tommy's truck's tires screeched to a stop as he slammed on the brakes. Tre was already jumping out of the passenger side door before it had come to a complete stop.

Rushing straight towards the nurse's desk, Tre immediately demanded answers. "I'm here looking for Nicear Jackson," he asked, hands braced on top of the desk.

After typing on the computer, the nurse read off the information. Before she could finish, Tre ran off, headed towards the double doors. Walking up to another information station in that area, Tre was greeted by Shelly Mack. Spotting blood all over her sent him into rage mode.

"What the fuck! Are you okay?" he shouted, scanning her body.

"I'm fine, it's not my blood," Shelly Mack assured him.

"Where's Nice?"

"He's in room 1122," Shelly Mack pointed.

Walking towards the room, Tre prepared himself for the worst. He and Nice had been friends since back when Tupac was dancing with Digital Underground. Once in the room, he was relieved to see Nice arguing with the nurse.

"Sir, you have to remain still or you're going to bust the stitches back open," the nurse was pleading.

"Come on, homie, let the lady do her job," Tre said.

Looking up, Nice was pleased to see his homie. Right when he was about to say something, Tommy came busting in, scaring the nurse half to death. She accidentally poked Nice's shoulder wound.

"Fuck!" Nice yelled.

"I'm so sorry, sir," the nurse said as she looked up at Tommy.

"Son, you cool?" Tommy asked with anger written all over his face.

"I'm cool, my nig. It went in and out," Nice replied, referring to his wound.

"Word is bond. I'ma murder everything moving," Tommy barked.

"Cool out, big homie. This is not the time nor the place," Tre told him, glancing at the scared nurse.

Walking into the room, Detective Smith scanned the three of them.

"Well, well, well, if it ain't Tre, Nice, and Tommy. This wouldn't, by any chance, be drug-related now, would it?" Smith asked.

Tre frowned when he saw the detective standing there.

"What the fuck you doing here?" Tre asked.

"Last time I checked, I was a cop," Smith replied.

"A crooked one, that is," Nice added.

"So I guess that means you won't be giving any statements?"

"I didn't see nothing, and I don't know nothing," Nice replied with a deadly stare.

"Fine. It makes no difference. I hope all you sons of bitches kill each other," Smith said with a smirk on his face.

"Excuse me, nurse, are you about finished?" Nice asked.

"Yes, sir, you just have to fill out a few papers and I'll be back with your pain medicine," she replied.

"Can you hurry up, please, 'cause I can't stand pork," Nice remarked, ice-grilling Detective Smith.

"Y'all assholes will slip up. And when y'all do, I'll be there," Smith assured them.

The hairs on Tommy's back were standing up as he stared down at Smith. If it wasn't for that badge hanging around his neck, Tommy would have closed that big mouth of his.

Sensing Tommy's anger and now wanting him to do anything foolish, Tre placed his hand on his shoulder.

"Cool it, big homie," he said.

With a smirk on his face, Detective Smith turned and head out of the room.

CHAPTER 23: FOR EVERY ACTION, THERE'S A REACTION

Retaliation was in the air of the stash house. Tre, Tommy, and Nice discussed what took place last night on Market Street. Nice explained to them every piece of detail.

"Man, I'm telling you, if it wasn't for little cuz, I probably wouldn't be here talking to y'all now. How the fuck was I caught slippin' like that!" Nice yelled in anger.

"Word, yo, don't even sweat that shit. Niggas gonna pay dearly, trust," Tommy assured him.

"Do you have any idea who might have done this?" Tre asked.

"I don't know who the fuck just signed their death wish," Nice replied.

"My nig, I'm about to apply pressure on the street. Someone knows something," Tommy said. "Until we find out who's behind this, we have to tighten our shit up. We can't allow nothing like this to happen again," Tre said, pulling out three bullet-proof vests.

"Now we're talking," Nice said, grabbing one.

"My dude, this shit is mad small," Tommy protested, holding up one.

142

"You got the wrong one," Tre laughed, passing him the biggest one.

"Man, tell Shelly Mack if there's anything she need, let me know, 'cause I owe her my life," Nice said, meaning every word.

"Homie, she did that for GP," Tre assured him.

"Fuck! What am I going to do about my truck?" Nice asked.

"Fuck it, get whatever money you're going to get out of it," Tre explained.

"Damn. I got to get a new one soon," Nice replied.

"Don't sweat it, I got the perfect person," Tre informed him before grabbing his cell phone.

*****

Lolling at his desk, Detective Smith was daydreaming of a young female he fucked last night when the Captain approached him.

"Smith! Are there any leads yet on the shooting on Market Street?" the Captain yelled, startling him.

"No sir. The victim won't talk and the witnesses at the crime scene are too scared to say anything," Smith informed him.

"Well, get me something or someone. All this violence is causing the higher-ups to bring pressure down on me," the Captain replied before walking off.

I'll give you someone, alright Smith thought.
He had the perfect person in mind. As soon as he handled things with Tre and his crew, he was going to bring down C-low's arrogant ass.

*****

Murda Mike was in a rage after hanging up from his phone conversation. He stormed from out of City Blue's, inside of Tri-State Mall. Hearing the word on the street had him on rampage mode. Tommy wanted to know who had anything to do with the shooting and was applying a lot of pressure on people.

Murda Mike was no punk, but far from a dummy too. If word was to get back to Tommy that they had anything to do with it, it would be a bloody war on the streets. Hopping into his Lexus, Murda Mike sped to the trap house on Pine Street.

There, he paced back and forth with his pistol in the palm of his hand.

"I still don't understand! How the fuck y'all ain't dead'em?"

"Some bitch came out of nowhere blasting on us," Skippie told him.

"You should have dead him and that bitch!" Murda Mike replied, feeling as if they were making excuses.

"You want us to try again?" Smooth asked.

"No, stupid, they will be waiting for that. We'll wait, yup, for the perfect time, then we will strike again," Murda Mike assured them.

Scanning the table, he noticed they were making bags of crack too big.

"What the fuck! Y'all trying to put a nigga out of business?" he snapped, holding up one of the pre-wrapped bags.

"We was thinking that we could move it faster if the bags were bigger," Smooth said.

"I don't pay y'all to think. Now do that shit right!" he ordered before walking upstairs.

Murda Mike ingressed into the bedroom, startling Sherry. Lifting her head up, he could clearly see the cocaine all over her nose. Walking over to her, he dropped his pants. Sherry stared up at him like he was a God and she was his servant.

The time he spent in prison did justice to his well-built frame. He kind of favored the rapper 'Baby' from Cash Money Records. Grabbing a hold of him, she handled his beefcake like an expert as her tongue moved ferociously over the tip of his penis.

Ordering her to turn around, he drilled her back side like an animal. High and numb, Sherry couldn't feel the pain he was applying. At the point of exploding, he pulled out, releasing himself all over her back side. Turning around, she sucked the remaining cum off of him.

"Ahhh... shit, bitch," he cried out in pleasure as he snatched away. Still with his pants down, he walked over to the dresser where Sherry once was and stuck his face in the small pile of coke. Lifting his head up, he looked like the guy from a scene off of the movie, 'Scar Face.'

He picked up the habit while on the inside, even after he'd sworn once that if he left prison, he would leave it alone. But being around Sherry brought his habitual self back out of him. Sprinkling some more coke onto his penis, he turned back towards Sherry.

"Round two," he said, flexing his muscles...

*****

Cream was in the hotel kitchen doing the damn thing. She was frying up some fish fillets and making some collard greens with oven-baked Macaroni cheese. One thing her mom sure taught her before she passed away was how to cook. As she flipped one of the fillets, her cell phone began ringing.

"Hello," she answered, keeping an eye on the frying fish.

"Bitch! You been M.I.A. What the fuck is going on!" Slow Juice shouted.

"Daddy, it's not like that. Let me explain," she replied nervously.

"Explain what! Peaches explained everything," he responded.

"Well, daddy--"

"Fuck all that. Did you find out anything or not?" he asked, cutting her off.

"Yes, daddy."

"Good, 'cause yo brother will be up there in a couple of weeks. Give the layout to him," Slow Juice ordered.

"Okay, daddy," she replied.

"And, Cream?"

"Yes?"

"Don't fuck up," he replied before hanging up.

Looking at her cell phone, Cream was confused and pissed. The loyalty she had for Slow Juice and her feelings for Nice weren't adding up.

"Fuck!" she screamed, throwing her cell phone down.

*****

Rushing from out of the shower, Tre answered his cell phone without checking the screen.

"Hello?"

"Mmm! I see you finally answering your phone now," a female voice spoke.

Checking his caller ID, Tre realized who it was.

"Bitch, what the fuck do you want? I know that was yo retarded ass who flattened my tires!" Tre barked.

"Fuck you and them tires! Next time, it will be worse," she threatened.

"Play yourself if you want, bitch, and your ass will be floating in the Delaware River."

"Nigga, you ain't going to do shit. The same thing happened to Nice's ass can easily happen to you too," she warned.

"What, bitch?" Tre snapped.

"Yeah, I'll be yo bitch, but I'm not the one Murda Mike got shook," she replied before hanging up.

On her side, Murda Mike appeared out of nowhere, "Bitch, who you talking to?" he asked, scaring the shit out of her.

"Nobody," she lied, looking over her shoulder.
Seeing him standing there with his dick in his hand, she knew what time it was.

*****

Throwing his cell phone down, Tre was pissed. His mind was replaying what Sherry had just said. If there was any truth in it, why would Murda Mike place a hit out on Nice? His instincts told him something wasn't right. Picking up his cell phone, he called Nice and Tommy, informing both of them to meet him at the stash house.

Sitting at the table with his hands crossed, Tre explained to them what Sherry said. The three of them sat in silence, in deep thought, looking puzzled.

"Why the fuck would Murda Mike want you dead?" Tre asked, breaking the silence between them.

"Fuck! Remember them little niggas I hit up a few months back?" Nice stated.

"Yeah, but what do that got to do with anything?" Tre questioned.

"One of them little niggas was his little brother," Nice informed him.

"You knew this the whole time and didn't tell me?" Tre asked.

"I didn't think it was a biggie. I mean the nigga was doing a bid," Nice responded.

"Key word, 'was,' and don't he fuck with them niggas Smooth and Skippie?" Tre asked.

"Them probably was the two who was shooting at me," Nice replied with anger.

"Fuck all of that, B. Them niggas want to play gangsta, I'ma show them gangsta," Tommy pressed, clinching his .50 caliber.

"Chill out, Tommy. Let's think for a second," Tre said. In deep thoughts, Tre came up with the perfect person for the job.

"I got it," Tre said, reaching for his cell phone.

"Hello?" a female answered.

"What's good, cuz?" Tre asked.

"Nothing really, just smoking some of that good-good."

"Listen, cuz. I can't talk over the phone. But I need you," Tre told her.

"That bitch ain't fucking wit you again, is she?" she barked.

"Nah, it's deeper than that. I'll explain later."

"Say no more, I got you," Shelly Mack replied.

As Tre hung up the phone, he thought for a second while Nice and Tommy looked at him, perplexed.

"What's good?" Nice was the first one to speak, not understanding what just happened.

"See, unlike us, Shelly Mack has a pussy, and with that power, she's going to lead Murda Mike to a secluded area. While me and her is taking care of him, you and Tommy will be taking care of Smooth and Skippie's asses," Tre schooled them.

"I'm feeling the move, son," Tommy stated.

"Yeah, me too, my nig," Nice added, now knowing how perfect Tre's plan was.

"After we get the drop on them niggas, we strike them were it hurts," Tre said. With that said, the three of them exited the stash house and jumped into their vehicles.

Sitting in his rental car, Nice grabbed a blunt that was already pre-rolled with exotic weed. Lighting it up, he took deep pulls. After allowing what they just discussed to sink in, he pushed number four on his CD player. The late great Tupac filled the air.

"Revenge is like the sweetest joy next to getting pussy" was all you heard as he pulled away.

CHAPTER 24: 1, 2, TRE & SHELLY COMING FOR YOU,
3, 4, NICE & TOMMY AT YOUR DOOR

Murda Mike bobbed his head as the two cruised up route 202. Shelly Mack eyed his every movement as he sipped from the pint of Hennessey. He reached out his hand and grasped her soft inner thigh. Her heartbeat pounded, her nostrils flared. But still in all, she faked a smile, placing her hand on top of his. She moved his hand closer towards her love peach as her tongue caressed her lips.

A few headlights behind, the death angel was lurking; Tre kept a hawk-eye on the two.

Over the past few days, Shelly Mack was all over Murda Mike like white on rice. Murda Mike couldn't shake the fact that he wanted her pretty behind as well. Tonight he was going to get more than he expected. Once in the parking lot, Murda Mike was anxious to get inside of her jeans and feel the warmth of her juices. The tight skinny jeans she was wearing weren't making the situation any better.

Then again, that was part of her plan and so far, her plan was working.

Tre parked in the distance as he watched them enter the hotel from the front. Loading his gun, he scanned the parking lot while waiting patiently. Inside Homewood Suites Hotel, Murda Mike and Shelly Mack were now entering room 123 on the first floor. Scanning her surroundings, she made a note of the suite. Standing on the heels of her shoes, she was exposing her ass even more.

"I'ma tear that ass up," Murda Mike said, smacking her on her back side.

"They all say that," she replied, adding an extra bounce in her walk. Strutting straight towards the master bedroom suite, she flopped down onto the bed. Coming right up from behind her, Murda Mike started fondling her.

"Hold on, sweetie, can a girl freshen up first?" she protested.

"A little funk won't hurt," he replied, trying to kiss her neck.

"I don't know what type of girls you into. But I like my pussy fresh," she responded, spreading her legs wide open. Doing that only made him want her even more.

"Hurry up, a nigga got moves to make," he ordered.

The only moves you'll be making, is to see your maker she thought, hopping up and exiting the room. Closing the bathroom door, she ran the water before texting Tre.

Just like a police stake-out, Tre was waiting patiently when he received the text. After checking his pistol and scanning the area one more time, he emerged from the stolen vehicle.

Exiting the bathroom, Shelly Mack noticed Murda Mike had his face down. Using this opportunity to her advantage, she slipped into the living room area towards the window. Once the window was unlocked and slightly ajar, she walked back

151

towards the bedroom. Sensing someone was watching him, Murda Mike lifted his head only to see Shelly Mack standing there, looking sexy as hell, wearing matching panties and bra.

"About time," he pouted, clearing his nose of any coke residue.

"Fucking junkie," she thought as she stood in front of the bed. Spotting his pistol on the night stand, she started dancing seductively. Laying back now with his penis in hand, he was beginning to grow impatient.

"Fuck all that dancing shit and come dance on this big dick," Murda Mike barked, stroking himself.

"I got something you can dance with," Tre snarled as he emerged from the doorway.

Looking from Shelly Mack to Tre back to Shelly Mack, Murda Mike knew what time it was. He was pissed with himself for allowing his self to be caught off-guard like this.

"You fucking bitch!" he shouted, reaching for his pistol. But he was too slow. Before he could get his hands onto his pistol, Shelly Mack was already unloading two rounds from her Ruger 22, silencer attached.

"Ahhhhhhhh! Bitch! You shot my dick! Ahhh! Fuck!" Murda Mike cried out in pain.

"It wasn't nothing there to begin with. You talking about a big dick. Nigga, please," she replied, smirking.

"Y'all better kill me, 'cause if not, y'all be dead by morning," Murda Mike yelled, still grabbing his crotch area.

"Your wish is my command," Tre said, emptying the clip into his body.

Looking over at Shelly Mack, Tre spoke. "Get dressed and wipe down everything you touched," he said, while calling Nice.

Nice answered on the first ring, "What's the verdict? "

"The head is gone, now get rid of the body," Tre spoke, referring to Smooth and Skippie.

"Say no more," Nice replied before hanging up.

Taking his time and checking everything, Tre made sure everything was cool. He wasn't worried about anybody hearing the gunshots either, 'cause, just like Shelly Mack, he, too, had a silencer screwed onto his gun.

"What about the cameras?" she asked.

"Don't sweat that, cuz. Homewood Suites don't have any," he assured her as they exited through the window.

*****

The block was dead with the exception of a few junkies standing on the corner. Looking over at Tommy, Nice confirmed everything was a go.

"Yo, son, you sure your shoulder is going to go through this?" Tommy asked.

"Man, shit, I popped two yellow bananas. Trust me, I don't feel shit," Nice assured him, referring to the two Percocets he had just washed down twenty-five minutes ago. Adjusting their hats and vests and checking their guns, they were ready for action.

"Son, how I look?" Tommy asked.

"Like the fucking police," Nice responded, not feeling the attire they were wearing. The two were dressed like ATF agents, and from the outside looking in, a person could have sworn they were the real deal.

Exiting the vehicle, they approached the front door. Nice stood next to the door and could hear noises coming from the inside. Giving Tommy the eye signal, he let him know that they were right on the other side of the door. Tommy signaled Nice to step aside. In one swift motion, Tommy kicked the whole door off the hinges.

"This nigga just kicked the whole door frame down," Nice mumbled as he moved right behind Tommy.

Thinking it was a drug bust, Smooth and Skippie both jumped up from the couch trying to attempt escape. With his .50 cal in hand, Tommy unloaded on them as they tried to flee. Smooth went down hard, but Skippie was still on the move. Nice chased after Skippie. Spotting him running out the back door, he picked up the pace. In the process of trying to hop the fence, Skippie's jeans got caught up on it. Hearing fate approaching, Skippie turned around, only to meet a bright spark sending him to his maker.

Now that will be a closed casket Nice thought as he turned and headed back into the house. Inside, Smooth was begging for his life. "Come on, man! What is it, money you want? Please don't kill me!"

"Damn, son, die with some dignity!" Tommy barked as he stood over him. The sign of Tommy's face had him scared out of his mind, but he still tried his best to convince him to spare his life.

"Listen, man. I can help you get at Murda Mike! Just please don't kill me!" Smooth pleaded, bleeding profusely.

"It's too late for all of that; he's already dead," Nice spoke as he entered the room.

"Please, I was just following orders. Don't do this, I have kids," Smooth begged.

"Son, they'll just have to grow up fatherless," Tommy snarled before pumping round after round into his chest area.

"We got to bounce, my nig," Nice said. The two of them exited the house at top speed. Hopping into a stolen vehicle, all that was left was skid marks as they fled the scene.

Meanwhile, upstairs, scared out of her mind, Sherry paced back and forth. She heard all of the gunshots and thought they were going to kill her next. After seeing Tommy and Nice pull off, she grabbed all the drugs and money she could before fleeing the house...

*****

The next morning, sitting at his desk, Detective Smith was getting chewed out by his Captain.

"Three murders! In one night! I need some answers, Smith, and I mean some God DAMN ANSWERS NOW!" he yelled, slamming down the local part of the paper.

"Sir, I'm on it. Trust me, I have everything under control." Just then a black woman in her early thirties came strolling in.

"Yes, Smith, and to make sure you're on top of it, I'd like you to meet your new partner, Detective O'Neal," the Captain introduced.

"Partner! No disrespect to you, O'Neal, but Captain, I don't think this is called for," Detective Smith said in defense.

"Smith, O'Neal is from New York and she was the top detective in her department. I strongly believe she will be a great asset to this department."

"But, Captain--"

"Don't 'but Captain' me. My decision is final," the Captain said, cutting Smith off. Facing O'Neal, he pointed to her new desk before walking off, leaving the two to get to know each other.

"So, you were the top detective in your department, huh?"

"Yes," O'Neal replied, moving a few papers around on top of her new desk.

"We'll see about that," Smith said, picking up the phone.

CHAPTER 25: THE BEGINNING OF A BEAUTIFUL RELATIONSHIP

Patrolling the city, Detectives Smith and O'Neal were out looking for some answers. Heading towards the north side of the city, Detective Smith was looking for a snitch. Not just any snitch, but the top snitch of them all. Turning down 17th street, Smith was creeping up as he looked from left to right.

"So, who's the perp?" O'Neal asked, breaking the silence.

"Yaps," Smith replied nonchalantly.

"Yaps! What type of name is that?" she wondered.

"You'll see," Smith assured her. Approaching the end of the block, Smith spotted his stool pigeon.

"Bingo," he said as he hopped the curb and jumped out. Before Smith's two feet could touch the pavement, Yaps took off running.

"Don't make me chase you!" Smith yelled while in pursuit with O'Neal hot on his trail.

Yaps hit the alleyway like a track star, but his speed was no match for O'Neal. The difference was that O'Neal used to be a track star in college before joining the force and could run faster than anyone. Passing Smith with ease, O'Neal took Yaps down hard.

Falling face first, Yaps tasted nothing but gravel. Jamming her knee into the back of his neck, O'Neal had him jacked up 'New York' style.

"Police brutality! Police brutality!" Yaps yelled.

"Shut up, you little punk," O'Neal replied, giving him a quick rabbit punch to the lower back.

"Ahhh! Fuck!" he cried out in pain.

Catching up and out of breath, Smith was pissed. Never in his sixteen years on the force had he thought he would be outdone by a female.

"Long...time...no see?" he said, still trying to catch his breath.

"Man... what you want from me, I didn't do shit!" Yaps said.

"You right, you didn't, but you know who did," Smith replied. Crouching down, Smith came within eye view, "Three murders took place last night. Who was involved and why?"

"Man, I don't know nothing," Yaps lied.

Pulling a sandwich bag filled with crack from out of his pocket, Smith swung it back and forth in front of his face. "Now you wouldn't want to be charged with this, would you?" he taunted.

"Man, this is some bullshit! You know that ain't mines," Yaps protested.

"Who's going to believe that, with a record like yours? I can definitely make it stick," Smith told him.

"OK," Yaps muttered.

"What? Speak up!" Smith barked.

"I said okay! Damn, what you want to know?"

"Stop playing games with me and spill it," Smith ordered.

"All I know is that them T-N-T niggas had something to do with it. I heard it was all over the young boy Nice shot a while back. Come to find out that young boy was Murda Mike's little bro. And when Murda Mike came home and found out, he placed a hit out on Nice. And since he didn't finish the job, the T-N-T niggas did," Yaps blurted out, his mouth moving a thousand miles per hour. O'Neal now knew why his name was Yaps.

"Slow down, so what you telling me is that all the shit that's been going down as of lately, is related?" Smith questioned.

"Yeah, man."

"Those mothafuckers. Good job," Smith said, before placing the sandwich bag on the ground in front of him.

"Man, I thought you said you wasn't going to charge me," he said, eyeing the sandwich bag of crack.

"I'm not. That's yours," Smith replied.

"Thanks, yo. Now can you tell this robo bitch to get up off of me?"

"That's Ms. Robo bitch to you," O'Neal retorted, smacking him in the back of his head before rising to her feet.

Not liking the fact that he was outdone by O'Neal, Smith had to admit he liked her style. It was the beginning of a beautiful relationship as the two new partners exited the alleyway.

*****

Tre, Nice, and Tommy were now driving south on I-95, heading towards Newport News, Virginia. It was also known as 'Bad News VA', the home of Allen Iverson, better known as 'Bubba Chuck.'

159

Following the directions exactly as C-low gave them, Tre got off the exit and headed towards uptown Denbigh. The Chop Shop that he was looking for sat right off of Warwick Blvd., right around the corner from the notorious 'Aqueduct Projects.' As they pulled up to the huge garage, they were greeted by vicious pit bulls on chains. Picking up his cell phone, Tre dialed Ace's number.

"What's good?" Ace answered on the second ring.

"Yo, it's Tre. I'm out front."

"Here I come now," Ace responded.

When the side door of the garage opened, they noticed a male with a fade and a part like the rapper Nas on his head.

Exiting the vehicle, they approached Ace.

Tre was the first to speak. "Ace?"

"Yeah, and you're Tre, right?" Ace replied with precaution.

"Yeah," Tre replied.

"What's good? Los told me a lot about you," Ace told him.

"Who?" Tre questioned, never hearing that name before.

"My fault, C-low. But I call him Los."

"Oh yea, he told me a few things about you as well. And this here is Tommy and Nice. Nice is the one with the car trouble," Tre said, introducing Nice.

"What's good? Yeah, come on in so that we can get down to business," Ace said, leading the way into the garage.

The inside of the Chop Shop looked like some Fast and Furious stuff. From the outside, you would have never expected there to be as many cars as there were on the inside. Ace had cars and trucks stashed everywhere, even up in the air.

"So, what is it you're looking for?" Ace asked Nice, scanning the area.

160

"Well, I just had the Escalade ESV. So something on the lines of that."

"I got that cocaine white Infinity Qx56, that big boy shit. It seats eight people comfy and you can place twenty-sixes on that mafucka. What you want to do?" Ace asked, pointing at the SUV.

Looking over the Qx56, Nice asked, "Can you make it bulletproof?"

"My nig, I'll make the mafucka bombproof if you want."

"Nah, bulletproof would be just fine," Nice replied.

Pointing to one of his workers, Ace ordered him to replace the windows with bulletproof glass and to add plates into the door's panel.

"So, what's the damage on that?" Nice asked, referring to the price of the SUV.

"Yo, you trying to grab a few drinks? Like fifty gees, it's going to be some sexy females there too," Ace told them.

Ace was the kind of guy that talked outside the scope, in fear that people were listening. He was a smooth guy, looking like he did nothing but get money and have sex all day. Believe it, he wasn't the type of guy you would want around your female. He had the cars, the money, the looks, and the charisma.

"Yeah, we could do some drinks," Tre told him.

"Good. It's going to take a few hours." Facing his worker, he said, "Place a twenty-three screen in the back."

Turning back to Nice, he said, "That one was on the house."

Looking back at Tre, Nice said, "I like this guy" as they exited the Chop Shop.

Twenty-five minutes later, the group was at 'Liquid Blue' strip joint. Inside was off-the-chain, some of the sexiest females, with the most plumpish behinds Virginia had to offer, dancing. Sitting down on the wrap-around couch, Ace, Tre, Nice, and Tommy were doing it up real big. They had bottles of Rose', Moet and Ace of Spade all over the table.

The strippers were really doing their thing too. To say that Tre and them were making it rain was an understatement. The way the strippers were making it clap, they made it pour on their asses. The staff and strippers was showing them major love out of respect for Ace.

In Wilmington, Delaware, they ran things, but down here in Bad News VA, it was Ace's world.

Out of Tommy's peripheral, he noticed a sexy, light-skinned female. "Damn, son, who's that bitch?"

Looking in the same direction, Ace noticed it was Jada. Jada was the baddest female in the strip joint. She was light-skinned and had a low haircut with golden streaks. Not to mention her body made men drool over it.

"A big guy, she likes what we like," Ace informed him.

"Damn, she goes both ways?" Tommy asked, hoping that she did.

"Nah, she's strictly clicky," Ace assured him.

"Damn," Tommy replied, but he really wasn't trying to hear that; he wanted Jada. He continued eyeing her as she climbed up onto the stage. T. Pain's 'I'm in love with a stripper' blared through the speakers.

Jada eyed the skinny pole like it was her pride and joy. With a sexy walk, she strutted towards the pole while moving to the beat. She worked her moves, making love to the pole as if it were her partner. Tommy made his way towards the front stage. Males and females were now making it rain onto the stage. Climbing up the pole, she swirled down slowly while sucking on her index finger. Dropping to her knees, she crawled like a horny feline towards Tommy. Jada loved how he hawked at her, and from what she could tell, he had plenty of money. The closer she got, the more Tommy's mind was made up. He wanted Jada; he didn't care what it took. He was up for the challenge.

Hours had passed and now back at Ace's Chop Shop, Nice was scoping out his new ride. He was feeling the fact that it had a safe hidden in the floor panel with a digital keypad. Out the corner of his eye, a blue Rolls Royce caught Tre's attention.

"How much is that blue shit running?" Tre asked.

"You talking about that Pepsi blue Rolls Royce Phantom. That's the new Drop Head Coupe, that mafucka come standard with suicide doors, V12 engine and some mo shit. That shit gonna hit you for damn near half a mil unless you get it from me. Ha! Ha!" Ace told him.

"I'm gonna have to take you up on that offer on the next trip down," Tre informed him.

"For you, Tre, I'll make it real special. Any friend of Los is a friend of mines," he replied.

Ace was feeling Tre; it was something about him he liked. After a few hand daps and making sure all the paperwork was legit, they were now back on I-95 heading north now in two vehicles.

CHAPTER 26: I'M IN LOVE WITH A STRIPPER

The next day, Nice was out showing off his new Infinity Qx56 as he drove down South Street looking for a parking spot. It was the weekend and there were mega sales everywhere so he figured it wouldn't hurt spending some money on himself and, of course, Cream, too.

"There goes a parking spot right there," Cream pointed out. After parking and placing some change into the parking meter, they were on their way to begin their shopping spree. It was chilly outside, but that didn't stop the hundreds of people that crowded the street.

"A', a lot of females be going here copping shoes. If you want, we can go and check it out," Nice offered, pointing towards the store.

Once inside the store Cream lit up like a Christmas tree. It was every woman's dream come true, like they were in 'Shoe Heaven.' It had all sorts of shoes, styles, and low prices. Rushing down the rows, Cream snatched up all types of shoes that sparked her interest.

"Excuse me, can you help me find sizes in these shoes? Hello? Excuse me!" she said it out loud to the young sales rep, who was rudely ignoring her. Looking in the direction she was looking, Cream noticed what had her attention...Nice.

"Now, see, that fine ass nigga over there is my man. So since you know that now, do you think yo ass can help a bitch?" Cream yelled, making her presence known.

"I wasn't looking at your man, honey," the sales rep replied, obviously upset that she wouldn't be able to get her flirt game on with Nice's fine ass.

"Whatever, just here. I need these in size six," Cream said before walking back towards Nice.

"You sure is getting a lot of attention," she pouted, standing with her hands on her hips.

"Damn, what I do?" Nice asked, grabbing her by the hand.

I'm fucking tripping. I get more attention than a motha-fucka. I'm a stripper for God's sake. This nigga got me open Cream thought.

Feeling all the stares from the other women, Nice knew what was up.

"Cut that out, Cream, fuck them hoes. Here, look," he leaned in and kissed her right on the spot. A sexual sensation went through her body as her knees became weak. "Now see, them bitches know you got me," Nice said, rubbing down her arms.

Cream was feeling like a school girl on her first day of school as all the attention was on her.

"Yup, this nigga definitely got a bitch wide open," she thought.

After paying for her shoes, the two continued on with their shopping. They hopped from store to store and six hours later, they were on their fourth trip back to the truck with more shopping bags in hand.

"You hungry?" Nice asked, helping her with the bags.

"Hell yeah," Cream replied.

"Good, I know the perfect place," Nice told her, helping her into the truck.

Once inside the truck, Nice searched through his CD case looking for a certain CD. Before placing it in, he busted open a strawberry Dutch master and filled it with some of his new batch of exotic. Reaching for his Bic lighter, he fired up his perfectly rolled blunt before pushing in the CD.

Within seconds, 'I'm in Love with a Stripper' lyrics by T-Pain were thumping for all to hear. All Cream could do was smile, but on the inside, she was crying. Ever since she was molested at an early age by her mother's boyfriend, she looked at men differently. She never thought love existed for her and thought that all men only wanted one thing - sex. So she used what her mother gave her and started stripping for a living. Now, Cream was feeling a feeling she thought didn't exist; a feeling she had trained herself for years to never have. But now she had it and it was scaring the shit out of her.

Why the fuck did I have to fall in love with this man? And to top it off, I fell in love with a man I can't even be with she thought as she grabbed the blunt from Nice.

Turning down the music, Nice spoke to her. "You know, you don't have to strip no more if you don't want to."

"I know, but why are you telling me this?"

"'Cause if you're going to be my girl, I don't want you stripping any more. Cream, I'll take care of you," he replied, looking into her eyes.

"Please, God, make him stop," she thought as a single tear slid down the side of her face.

"What's the matter? Did I say something wrong?"

"No... it's just.... I.... I just never met no one who really cared for me, that's all."

"I don't know why, as beautiful as you are, a man has to be a FOOL," he replied, wiping away her tears with his finger.

"That was sweet. Do you talk to all the females you date like this?" Cream replied before relighting the blunt.

"You want the truth? No. But with you, I can get used to saying things like that. Stick around and you'll see," he said, pulling off.

Easy for you to say she thought as she sat back, lost in her thoughts.

CHAPTER 27: HAPPY BIRTHDAY

It was December 4th and since the big come-up, Tre's money had been climbing up the ranks fast. Thanks to Tommy's coke connect and C-low's hustling expertise, Tre was now in a league of his own. His trips to Miami were far more frequent now that he and Casina were getting closer. Tonight was no different. When Tre entered the bedroom, he was looking good as ever, with canary diamond cufflinks blinging.

Sitting at the vanity mirror, Casina was applying her MAC cosmetics when she felt his presence behind her.

"Hi, sweetie," she said, applying the finishing touch.

"Hello, birthday girl," he responded in his Keith Sweat tone of voice. Walking up to her, he placed a platinum chain around her neck. With six hundred and twenty round diamonds total in her chain, Casina's mouth dropped as she touched the ten-carats hanging around her neck.

"Oh my God! Thank you so much, baby," she said as she spun around, looking glamorous in her Prada dress. It fit her like it was part of her skin. As she rose, their lips locked.

Tre had been showering her with expensive gifts and even took it as far as hiring an architect to redesign their condo.

Taking a step back, she asked. "Are you ready, baby?"

"Yes, sweetheart. The question is, are you ready?" Tre replied, savoring the smell of her perfume.

It's not you I'm worried about. It's my dumb ass brothers. "Yes, handsome, I'm ready. Let's go," she said, checking herself over one more time.

Ricky and Rayman put together a dinner party for her and tonight was the night Tre was finally going to meet them. Casina's mind was racing, her stomach turning just thinking about it.

As they were exiting the lobby, neither thought the paparazzi would be out.

"My daddy is going to be proud of me," she thought, hiding the camera and going back to work.

*****

Pulling up to the double-gated entrance, Casina reached over Tre and entered the codes to open the gates. Driving along the brick pavement, Tre was shocked when he came within eyesight of the Mansion.

Damn, this looks like some MTV Cribs shit he thought. It was clearly the biggest crib he had ever laid eyes on. There were palm trees everywhere and the landscape was evergreen. Tre also noticed there were guard dogs spread out around the property with armed men posted next to them.

"Damn, her brothers must be on some real live 'Scar Face' type of shit. Now this is how niggas is supposed to be living," he thought as they parked.

The inside was just as extravagant: you could tell it was designed by professionals. Spotting her brothers approaching, Casina became tense.

169

"Happy birthday, sis!" Ricky said as he walked up to her and gave her a hug.

Casina could smell the alcohol all over him. Tre studied the two men carefully. With a head full of dreadlocks, both were standing at six foot even. With a caramel complexion and athletic build, both were styling in the latest suits made by Tom Ford with iced-out cufflinks. If it wasn't for the scar on one, you wouldn't be able to tell them apart.

"Thanks," Casina replied.

"Happy 24th birthday, sis," Rayman said, leaning in and giving her a kiss on the cheeks.

"Thanks, Rayman. I would like y'all to meet my boyfriend, Tre," Casina introduced.

"Boyfriend, huh?" Ricky spat, before turning around and walking off.

"Don't mind him. It's nice to finally meet you," Rayman said, extending his hand.

"Nice to meet you too," Tre replied, accepting his handshake.

"Come this way, dinner awaits," Rayman informed them.

Following his lead, Tre and Casina walked side by side.

"Baby, if you feel uncomfortable at any time, we will leave. Just say the word," Casina told him.

"Sweetheart, it's your day. Let's see what dinner's hitting on first. And if things don't go well, then you can decide on our next move," he replied.

"Okay, baby," she said. Casina loved the fact that Tre was so understanding and dominant at the same time. Noticing that they were heading towards the ballroom and not the dining area, Casina grew suspicious.

Walking through the double doors, Tre and Casina noticed it was pitch dark. Tre cursed himself for not having a pistol on him. But that wouldn't have mattered anyway; he was checked by the guards before he stepped foot into the mansion.

"Rayman, what's going --"

Before she could finish her sentence, she heard, "SURPRISE!!!"

All of the lights came on. Casina was stunned to see the faces of her old high school and college friends. They were all smiling and clapping. Tre was shocked to see who was standing next to Lolita, grinning happily.

"I know, gurl, but your brothers told me not to say nothing. Happy B-day, gurl," Lolita said, giving her a gurly hug.

"Thank you, gurl," Casina replied with tears of joy in her eyes.

"Happy birthday, Casina," C-low said, giving her a hug as well.

"Thank you, C-low," she replied.

Tre looked at C-low, surprised that he wasn't let in on the secret surprise.

"Hey, homie, it was all her. I didn't know shit until the last minute," C-low said, as if reading Tre's thoughts.

"It's all good. Look at you. I didn't know you like to throw on that type of shit," Tre said, checking out his attire. C-low had on a black suit, cream shirt and a pair of cream socks, all made by Prada. He was definitely getting his grown man on, with his Prada shoes and icy chain hanging perfectly. By his side, Lolita was looking flawless and sexy as ever in her Prada dress, show-ing off her natural curves.

"Y'all two look so good together," Casina said, admiring them. She looked around. There were waiters and waitresses

171

serving Moet, Rose' and appetizers of all sorts to everyone. Looking to her left, Casina saw lights on the stage light up. Just when she thought it couldn't get any better, her favorite R&B singer appeared out of nowhere, singing his own version of 'Happy Birthday.'

Casina stood motionless as the vocals traveled through her body. Grabbing her by the hand, the singer sung to her like Eddie Cane from off 'Five Heartbeats.' A sense of jealousy came over Tre and not being able to take it anymore, Tre stole the attention by butting in and kissing Casina on the center stage. That was the icing on the cake: she exhaled as their tongues wrestled as if in a thumb war.

The anger in Ricky boiled over and he moved towards Tre and Casina. Just before he was within reach, he felt a hand on his shoulder. Turning around and ready to swing, Ricky noticed it was his brother.

"No, Ricky, let her enjoy herself. It's her day, remember?" he reminded him, giving him a stern look.

Hands down, Ricky was indeed a loose cannon, but Rayman could get just as crazy, if not worse. Brushing past his twin, Ricky walked towards the table and turned up a bottle of Rose'. Shaking his head, Rayman let his brother be. Turning back, he saw Casina standing before him.

"Thank you so... so... so much," she said, kissing him on the cheek and hugging him.

"You're welcome, sis, but you need to be thanking Ricky on that performer. You know I'm not too fond of what he did on that DVD. You know I seen that, right?"

"That wasn't him on there," Casina protested.

"How you know, you seen it?" Rayman questioned, raising his eyebrows.

Casina dropped her head. At the age of twenty-four, her brothers still had that effect on her.

"Hey, I 'm just playing," he said, trying to bring light to the situation. Just then, the R&B singer was back on center stage, singing one of his latest hits.

"Excuse me, sis, can I have this dance?" Rayman asked. The two of them got their party on. Casina was experiencing a side of Rayman she had never seen. For the first time ever, he was treating her like a lady and not a little girl. It was at that very moment she realized that Rayman shared a similar side as her father.

After the song, Rayman lead Casina over to the table where the bottles of champagne were. Grabbing the microphone from his pocket, Rayman signaled the DJ to kill the music.

"I like y'all to raise your champagne glasses in the air. If you don't have one, there are servers walking around with them," Rayman spoke.

After seeing everyone with a glass of champagne in hand, he spoke into the mic once again.

"I would like to make a toast to my beautiful sis. I know at times we can be hard on you, but believe me when I say it's all out of love. So with that said, happy birthday and many more," Rayman said while raising the bottle of Rose, in the air.

Before anyone could toast to Rayman's words, Casina had a toast of her own. Grabbing the microphone, she spoke. "First I want to say thanks to all of y'all for coming and I want to thank my brothers for putting this event together. I also want to thank my boyfriend for being there for me in a time of need. I would like to make an additional toast to true love," she said, raising her glass to Tre.

"True love! Yeah, right! What you know about some fucking true love!" Ricky blurted out.

The crowd turned in his direction, shocked by the words that just came out of his mouth.

"What is it, Ricky? Why can't I be happy? Rayman accepted my happiness, why can't you?" Casina yelled.

"'Cause it's not love, sis. You're blinded by this fool. I can smell a hustler a mile away. You deserve better, sis. That's all. It's plenty of good men out there. I don't want you to make the same mistake mom made by messing with dad!" Ricky shouted. He held his father responsible for their mother's death.

"What do you mean by 'mistake'? Daddy wasn't no mistake. He was a good man!" she yelled back.

True, she heard all the stories about her father and how he conducted business in the streets. But she didn't care. That was still her father and she loved him.

"What good man places his family in jeopardy? Thanks to our father, we have no family!" Ricky barked, staggering. He was deep in his feelings now, the alcohol doing all the talking. What he said was like a smack to her face.

"I hate you!" she screamed, charging at him like a bull. Not thinking clearly, Ricky shoved her down hard. Tre reacted to the situation by shoving him even harder. After helping Casina up, Tre turned and faced Ricky, ready to close that big mouth of his. C-low stood right by his side, ready for whatever was to come.

Regaining his composure, Ricky drew out his gun, aiming it directly at Tre and C-low. The guests went into a frenzy, trying to get out of the way. Even the famous R&B singer took cover.

"Nigga, if you're going to pull the trigger then pull it!" Tre barked.

Before Ricky could respond, Rayman stepped in front of them.

"It won't be none of that. Casina, are you okay?" he asked.

"Yes," she replied, tears cascading down her face.

"You and your friends get out of here. I'll deal with this situation with Ricky," Rayman assured her.

Tre was still ice-grilling Ricky when Casina pulled him away. Once they were out of eyesight, Rayman faced Ricky. Observing all the hurt in his eyes was enough said.

"You're wrong, Ricky" was all Rayman said before leaving Ricky there to deal with his demons.

CHAPTER 28: SEX ON THE BEACH

Casina sped down Collins Avenue in rage: she couldn't believe the stunt her brother had just pulled. It was supposed to be her night. She was supposed to be happy, but thanks to Ricky, it was now a disaster.

Tre sat in silence as he watched Casina vent. As fast as she drove, they were back at the Akoya in no time. After handing the car keys to the valet, they headed to the lobby.

Casina was on her way towards the elevator until Tre stopped her and turned her towards him.

"Baby, let's take a walk on the beach. I believe that's what you need to clear your mind."

"Okay, baby," she agreed. She loved the fact that Tre could make light of any situation.

Exiting through the back entrance of the Akoya, they were instantly on the beachfront. Before walking any further, they both removed their shoes. After walking a quarter of a mile down the beach, they stopped and stared out at the Atlantic Ocean. The view was like no other: the moon shined on the ocean waves like a spotlight, as if it was made to be a romantic setting.

Facing Casina, Tre placed his hand on her beautiful face and said, "It's okay now."

"I'm sorry for what happened tonight," was all she managed to say as tears began sliding down her face.

"You have no reason to feel sorry, sweetheart. That wasn't your fault," Tre told her, placing his signature kiss on her forehead.

"Tre, can I ask you a question?"

"Baby, you can ask me anything."

"What is it that you really do for money?" she asked, staring directly into his eyes.

Tre was caught off-guard; since they had been together, what he did for money was never the topic of discussion. Seeing the sincere look in her eyes, he felt the truth needed to be heard.

"Baby, what your brother said tonight was the truth. I'm a drug dealer, sweetie."

"I should have known. How could I be so stupid?" she replied, dropping her head.

"Casina, look at me. Look at me, baby. I'm sorry for not being completely honest with you."

Staring deep into his eyes, she was beginning to question everything about the man who stood before her, the man who she thought she knew.

"What are you trying to accomplish by hustling?" she spoke softly.

"The world and everything in it."

"So, in this world of yours, where do I fit in?" she reasoned. She had to make him see her in the picture.

"I don't know... I just know I want to be with you. I'm still trying to figure it all out."

"Maybe my brother was right about everything," she said, feeling as if she had been played for a fool.

"No, he wasn't, sweetie."

"What makes you say that? What makes you so different, Tre?"

"'Cause I'm willing to give it all up for you. Since I've met you, my life has changed. Before, I would never allow a woman to get this close to me. But with you, it's different. I realize now that there's more to life than this. You're not living life until you experience everything it has to offer. I thought I had it all until I met you, baby. You helped me see a different me, you showed me that love is a good thing. There's no other woman on earth I would rather spend the rest of my life with but you. And if that means for me to give everything up, then I will."

"You sure, Tre? You sure you love me that much?"

"Yes, I love you, Casina. See, baby, love is like a newborn child, and the most precious part about it is that you get the chance to watch it grow into something magical."

That was like music to her ears. "I love you, Tre," she said as they began to kiss. Without warning, Casina broke their kiss and took a step back. There was nobody in sight as she removed her dress. Following suit, Tre took off his shirt and laid it down on the sand. Laying her down onto his shirt, Tre studied his Nubian Goddess.

Her nipples were erect from the ocean breeze, the moonlight gave her body somewhat of a glow.

Opening her legs for better access, Tre began tasting her sweetness. Running his tongue along the outline of her pussy lips, then slowly licking her insides, sent a tingling sensation throughout her body. He sucked on her now-swollen clit while flicking his tongue over it. Arching her lower back, she moaned as she released her juices all over his lips and chin.

Lifting his head up, Tre stared at her beautiful face as he began to remove his pants. Her pussy welcomed his manhood with open arms. Her natural lubrication was making sweet love sounds as he stroked in and out of her mound. With lust in her eyes, she gripped his shoulders and began moving her Brazilian hips back and forth, allowing him to drive his manhood even deeper.

"Mmmmm... Sssss," she moaned. Her moans really made him throw his back into it.

"Ohhh! Ohhh my God, Tre.... I'm cumming again!" she screamed, but this time Tre wasn't too far behind her as he released a load of his own.

The two of them collapsed on their back, breathing heavily. Staring up in the sky, Casina was in a daze.

"Momma, if you're listening, please give me the strength to make this work and last. Please let this be the man of my dreams. With him present, it feels as though my life is complete. They say God always comes right on time. Well, I hope this is the right time, 'cause I sure do want it to be. And daddy, I know you're watching over me too. You would have loved Tre. The way he treats me reminds me of you. I love you, daddy, and I miss y'all so much. Please God, in Jesus's name, watch over us. Amen," she prayed silently.

Snuggling tight, there was no other place they would rather be than in each other's arms. That night they put a new meaning to having sex on the beach as they made love over and over again.

CHAPTER 29: I WANT OUT

Seated at the bar inside of the TGI Friday's located on Dupont Highway, Tre was deep in thought. Since his confession with Casina, he had been thinking about why he was still in the game. He had more than enough money and he had the woman of his dreams. So why stay in the game? What was the point?

"Sir, your total is twenty-nine dollars," the young waitress said, breaking his train of thoughts.

Reaching into his pocket, Tre peeled off a fifty-dollar bill and placed in on top of the counter.

"Keep the change," he said and rose from his stool, placing his fitted cap back on his head.

"Thank you so much, sir," the young waitress replied happily as Tre left the restaurant.

Sitting in his vehicle, Tre's mind was made up. He wanted out and nothing was going to stop him. He just hoped Nice and Tommy would understand.

"Fuck it, I'll just have them meet me at the stash house tonight, and I'll tell them then," he resolved. Casina had convinced him to change his life, and by all means he wanted the best for her.

Tre was in such a deep thought that he didn't notice he was being followed as he pulled out of TGI Friday's parking lot.

*****

She looked at her screen, pushing the end button once again. Since Cream's brother came to town, she had been avoiding Nice and his calls. She was really stuck between a rock and a boulder. She cursed herself for getting involved.

Slouched in the chair, Trap was getting corn rows placed in by Peaches. He was enjoying the taste of the exotic weed.

"Damn, sis, where you get this shit from?" he asked, exhaling the smoke through his nostrils.

Just knowing the answer to his question ate Cream up even more as she thought about the ounces of exotic weed Nice had given her just a few days ago.

"From someone I know," she replied nonchalantly.

"Cream, that's Nice's weed, ain't it?" Peaches said, a smirk on her face.

"Bitch, I should come over there and smack that smirk right off your face," Cream was thinking. Peaches really was starting to get up under her skin and she wasn't feeling her at this point.

"Why you fronting like this, sis?" Trap asked, standing up. At 5' 9", his brown-skinned skinny build made him look similar like O-Dog off the movie, Menace II Society.

"I'm not, I'm cool," Cream replied, still staring down Peaches. If looks could kill, Peaches would have died a thousand deaths.

"Good, then, program that address in there for me," he ordered her, tossing her the navigation device. "And make sure y'all pack everything tonight, 'cause we blowing this joint once it's done," he said before taking a few more pulls from the blunt.

*****

Later that night at the stash house, Nice and Tommy couldn't believe their ears. Tre had just broken the news to them about him wanting out the drug game.

"So now you want out!" Nice expressed, breaking the silence between the three.

"Listen, I just don't want to be doing this shit for the rest of my life!"

"Who the fuck are you? "

Tre turn his head sideways," What the fuck is that supposed to mean?"

"Exactly what I said, Cause the nigga that is standing in front of me, can't be the same nigga that I grew up with!" Nice spat.

"Chill, son, y'all two wildin'. Now, Tre, where's all this coming from? I thought we was in it to win?" Tommy interjected, trying to cool the tension building up between his two homies.

"You right! I'm winning, so I want out while I'm still a winner," Tre replied, staring Nice right into his eyes.

"Then what! You think you're going to live a regular life? You think the streets going to allow that?" Nice shouted, still not agreeing with Tre decision.

"Man, fuck the streets. It's more to life than them damn streets. I'm trying to build a future and maybe even have a family one day."

"Oh, I see what this is all about. It's about that bitch in Miami," Nice snapped, now knowing who was filling his boy's head up with the bullshit.

"Son, that's not cool. Leave his lady out of this," Tommy intervened.

"Nah, let him speak!" Tre barked, equally boiling with anger.

"Nah, Tommy right. I'm out of here. But you need to check yourself, Tre. Talking about fuck the streets. Nigga, WE ARE THE STREETS!!!" Nice yelled before storming out of the stash house.

Tommy's arm stopped Tre from going after Nice, "Listen, Tre, it's your life. If that's what you want, I support you, homie. Let Nice cool off. I'll talk to him."

Tre took a deep breath, "I hear you," he replied. Five minutes later, Tommy and Tre emerged from the house. Giving each other hand daps, the two hopped into their vehicles and went their separate ways.

Once the coast was clear, Detective Smith emerged from the shadows. He had been watching them for hours now, waiting for the perfect timing to catch them slipping. He didn't realize there was someone else waiting in the shadows too, trailing him.

This ought to slow them down for a while Smith thought, approaching the house with a slow stride. Using his police tactics, he was able to break in with ease. Once inside, he was moving around like a mad man. From the many previous drug busts, Smith knew all the right places to search. Before long, he had done a clean sweep of the house and found eight bricks of powder, three bricks of crack, and fifteen pounds of different types of exotic weed. *Damn, they were doing their thing; this should hold my young boys for a while* he thought, examining the drugs. After loading all of the drugs into a trash bag, Smith headed out the front door. Checking his surroundings, Smith proceeded towards his car.

Squatted incognito behind some bushes, a shadow popped up out of nowhere, nearly scaring the shit out of Smith. Lucky for him, he already had a gun in his hand.

"Freeze! Police!" Detective Smith yelled with his gun aimed.

"I don't know too many police dressed in all black, coming out of a stash house. Not to mention, no back up, with a trash bag filled with God knows what," Trap let it be known, aiming his two 9mm pistols, showing no sign of fear or backing down.

"Listen, kid, it's not what you thinking. No one has to get hurt here," Smith murmured, backing up slowly.

"I'm not your kid, so drop the bag, old man, or somebody is going to get hurt," Trap warned him as he clenched the grips of his pistols.

Still backing up, Smith stumbled and accidentally fired off a round, nearly missing Trap's head by inches. Trap wasn't used to being shot at; his street instincts kicked in. He unloaded round after round into Smith's body. Smith wished he was wearing his bullet-proof vest as he felt the bullets slamming into his body. But it was far too late for wishes: blood was already pouring out of his wounds.

Trap walked up to Smith as if he was the grim reaper. He was ready to finish what Smith had started. Towering over Smith's body, he could tell that he was fighting for his life and would be dead soon. Elevating his pistols, he wanted to hasten the process.

Two gunshots rang out from behind him. What Trap felt next slung him to the ground. Luckily for him, he was wearing a vest and he rolled back over, sending a few rounds of his own in the direction of the shots. Jumping back to his feet, Trap moved towards his vehicle while scanning the area.

Spotting somewhat of a shadow over by a car, Trap fired off a few more rounds before hopping in the car and fleeing the scene.

Smith laid there and watched as he saw the shadow approaching fast and screaming at a running figure. His vision was going blurry and hot blood was escaping his body at a rate faster than his weak heart could provide it.

Kneeling down, O'Neal couldn't believe her eyes. Grabbing her walkie-talkie, she called for backup.

"OFFICER DOWN! OFFICER DOWN! I REPEAT, OFFICER DOWN! THIS IS DETECTIVE O'NEAL! I'M ON 27TH AND WASHINGTON! BRING PARAMEDICS. HURRY!!!" she yelled.

She dropped her walkie-talkie and applied pressure on Smith's wounds.

"Hold on, partner! Help is on the way," she cried out.

Noticing his hand was clenched tightly to a trash bag she had seen him taking out of the house, O'Neal grew even more suspicious than she had first been. His funny acting had been the main reason why she had decided to follow him in the first place. Opening his trash bag after taking it out of his hands, her eyes couldn't believe what she saw.

What have you been into she thought as she looked from the bag full of drugs back to Smith.

But observing her partner's quick and hard breaths, she began pumping his chest with her hands, trying to clear his

185

lung's passage by giving him CPR. Little did she know it was too late for all of that.

The hard breaths she heard him taking so desperately, were Smith's last.

CHAPTER 30: THE HEAT IS ON

The next morning, Tre was awoken by loud banging and Psycho's barking. Checking his cell phone for the time, he noticed he had sixteen missed calls. Reaching for his pistol, he walked towards the door with precaution.

Peeping through the peephole, Tre noticed it was Tommy standing on the other side of the door with a newspaper in hand. Ordering Psycho to go to the backroom, he let his homie in.

"Damn, nigga, you going to break my door down?" Tre barked, letting him in.

"Son, we got a major fucking problem!" Tommy exclaimed, slamming the newspaper down.

"What the fuck do you mean?" Tre asked, picking up the local paper. As soon as he read the headlines, his question was answered.

The headline read, "A Detective was murdered late night in the city of Wilmington. Detective Smith, 41, of Bear, Delaware, was gunned down last night on the 27th and Washington Street. His partner, Detective O'Neal, was the first responder on the scene. A shootout occurred between her and the killer. We believe the killer is a young black male in his early twenties. He was last seen driving in a dark blue Chevy. He's also labeled armed and dangerous. The Department doesn't have a motive yet behind this attack, but they believe Detective Smith was coming out of 1232 address before being gunned down. Smith was a thirteen-year veteran of the Wilmington Police Department. He was a good cop and will be missed. The Wilmington Police Department is asking anyone with leads to please contact 302-555-5115."

"Fuck!" Tre shouted, balling up the newspaper and throwing it to the floor.

"Yeah, fuck is right. I rode past there earlier and mad po-po was everywhere," Tommy informed him.

"Man, this is some bullshit. How the fuck did this shit happen?" he questioned. He wanted answers.

"Son, I don't know, but our fingerprints are all over that crib. So the heat is definitely about to be on us," he told him, pacing back and forth.

"Hold up! They didn't mention anything about drugs in the paper. Why didn't they mention that? This isn't making sense. And who the fuck murdered Smith's bitch-ass? Are we being set up? And where the fuck is Nice's ass at?" he yelled. This was too much for him and things weren't adding up. Right when he wanted out of the game, he was pulled back in even deeper.

"I talked to son earlier; he's tripping just like us."

"Fuck! This is not supposed to be happening. Look, we have to prepare ourselves for the worst. I want y'all to secure y'all money, just in case things get shaky. Then we need to keep a low profile and see what type of things unfold and surface. The house wasn't in any of our names, but like you said, our prints are all over the place. You have somewhere to lay low until we figure out what's going on?"

"Yeah, I'll take Nice with me up to NY. We will be good up there," Tommy assured him.

"Cool, I'ma head down Miami. There ain't shit in my name. So I should be good down there. And before we route, we have to grab some throw-away phones, so that we can communicate with each other," Tre informed him.

After Tommy left, Tre went and bought a pre-paid phone. He contacted Casina, informing her that he would be down there tomorrow. Ending the call, he started putting things into play.

Tre had so much to do and too little time to do it. The heat was definitely about to be turned up; he just wanted to make sure he and his crew didn't get burnt in the process.

*****

Meanwhile, Back in Atlanta...

Slow Juice was pissed as he was working out; Trap just arrived and laid the bad news on him once again. He wasn't liking it one bit. That robbery was supposed to get things started for him and it was supposed to place him where he was supposed to be...On Top!

Finishing up his last rep, Slow Juice sat down the dumbbells and grabbed his water bottle. After a few sips, he grabbed a towel and wiped the sweat from his body. At the age of 38, you would have thought he was younger. Standing 5' 10", a buck ninety-five, light-skinned, with a temple tapered with waves, Slow Juice was a lady pleaser; the time spent behind the walls did his body justice.

"So let me get this straight, you feel me, we didn't get nothing!" he shouted.

"No, big homie," Trap replied, feeling bad for coming up empty-handed for the second time.

"And you, I ought to smack the shit out of you, you feel me!" Slow Juice barked, marching towards Cream. Before he was able to place his hands on her, there was a knock at the door.

"Who the fuck is it?" Slow Juice barked before removing his pistol from his waistband.

"It's me, daddy," a female voice said from the other side of the door.

Opening the door, Slow Juice was shocked to see who was standing before him.

"Star, what are you doing here? I thought you wanted out. I thought you was doing your own thing in Miami. What brings you back to the 'A'?" He allowed her to enter.

"I went down there chasing the wrong dream. Modeling is just not for me," she replied.

"So you think you can just come back to this family empty-handed, you kidding me?"

"No, daddy. I'm not empty-handed. I been doing my homework. And I got something good for you," Star informed him while handing him a yellow envelope.

Just like Peaches and Cream, Star also worked for Slow Juice before he went to the Feds. She used to help with planning the setups. Now that he was back out, she wanted to show her loyalty again.

"What the fuck is this?" he asked, opening up the envelope and pulling out some photos. Studying the pictures, he had no idea who or what he was looking at.

"What is this, Star? I don't have time for this shit, you feel me. I'm trying to make power moves, you feel me," he barked, throwing down the pictures.

"Daddy, that's what I'm trying to tell you. This nigga is holding. And the chick he's with, brothers is running Miami," she replied, hoping he would be pleased to hear that.
Trap glanced at the photos on the ground and immediately recognized the male in the picture.

"Big homie! That's the nigga right there!" he shouted, reaching for the pictures. Catching a quick look at the photo, Cream also knew who the male was. It was Tre, but she didn't know who the female in the photo with him was.

"What do you mean?" Slow Juice asked with a puzzled look.

"I mean, the nigga right here, in this picture. I seen him last night coming from out the stash house," Trap told him.

"Hold up, hold up, what you mean to tell me is that the same nigga Star been scoping out in Miami, is the same nigga you seen all the way up in Delaware?" he questioned.

"That's what I am saying, big homie," Trap replied.

"Are you sure?" Slow Juice asked again, not believing it. What were the chances that this was the same guy?

"Yeah, I'll never forget a face, big homie. A', wasn't Fat Cat's connect from Miami?" Trap asked.

Facing Star, Slow Juice demanded her to tell him everything she knew. If everything that was being said was true, then the stakes just went up.

After hearing her story, he was satisfied with what he heard. He came up with the perfect idea. Facing Trap, he laughed as he said, "We're going to Miami, you feel me."

"Miami?" Trap replied, turning his face sideways.

191

"Yeah, kidnap that bitch, you feel me," he laughed.

CHAPTER 31: KIDNAP THE BITCH

Enjoying the lyrics off her new Usher's track, Casina was cleaning her condo from head to toe. She was trying to get things in order before Tre got back home. He was due to arrive later and she had something special stored for him.

After she was finished cleaning, she found herself out on the balcony overlooking the city of Miami. Out of all the years in Miami, she had never imagined such a beautiful view. She was now seeing it fully. Knowing Tre was going to be by her side made this view even better.

I wish my mom and dad could have met Tre she thought and at that very moment, she fell apart. Tears of sorrow flowed down her cheeks.

Casina would never forget that dreadful day; it played in her mind over and over again. The words 'I love you, baby girl' were the last thing her father had said to her. Looking up into the blue sky, she said, "I love you too, Mommy and Daddy."
Feeling the presence of someone behind her, Casina smiled. "Honey, I thought your plane was due to arrive later. And why didn't you call me to pick you up? I know you didn't catch a cab," she said, quickly wiping her tears, her back still turned towards him.

"Damn, shawty, you don't have to cry," a male voice replied.

Realizing it wasn't Tre's voice she heard, fear overwhelmed her. Before she could turn around and face her intruder, he placed his arm around her neck and smothered a handkerchief over her nose and covered her mouth with the other hand. Casina panicked as she tried to put up a fight. But whatever chemicals the handkerchief was drenched in, blinded her vision and sent her to the la-la land.

"I thought we was supposed to kidnap her, not kill her," Star said.

"She's not dead, she's just in a deep sleep," Trap assured her.

"Oh," Star replied.

"Come on now and help me mess up the place a little so that we can get out of here," Trap said, knocking over a few things.

After everything was out of place and leaving a note behind, they exited the condo with precaution. Heading down the hallway towards the elevator, Trap carried Casina over his shoulder. Once the elevator door was open, Trap and Casina were the first to enter. Hearing someone approaching, Star took a step back, signaling Trap to keep quiet.

"A' Selena, you know if I got any mail?" a male voice asked.

"I don't know, sir, but as soon as I get downstairs, I will check on that for you," Star replied.

"Do that for me, sexy. I got to go to the studio later and I'm waiting for something to come through the mail," he said, walking back to his condo with a styrofoam cup in his hand.

"Damn, that was close," Star said, entering the elevator with Trap.

"Who was that?" Trap asked.

"One of those rapper guys," Star replied nonchalantly.

"Damn, you got some major players that stay up in this bitch, huh?"

"Yeah, you never know who you might run into," Star said with a smile. If it was under different circumstances, she would have tried to get with the brown-skinned, tattooed from the face down, long dreadlocked rapper. But this was business, and business came before pleasure.

The first part of the kidnapping was over. The next part was to get out of the Akoya unseen as they headed down to the garage level.

*****

Outside of Miami's International Airport, Tre was upset as he hopped into a cab. He had called Casina five times and there was still no answer. That was unlike her and he wanted to know what was up.

"Maybe she's sleep," he thought to himself.

"Where to?" the cab driver asked, checking his meter.

"The Akoya," Tre replied as he sat back in deep thought.

Thirty minutes later, Tre was riding the elevator up to his floor, trying to come up with a solution to his problem. He wanted to know why and who was behind the murder of Detective Smith.

Opening the door, Tre's heart dropped when he saw the place in disarray. He knew that could mean only one thing: it had been vandalized.

"What the fuck!" he thought, moving towards the bedroom.

"Casina! Casina! Baby, where are you?" Tre panicked as he rushed into the bedroom.

Rushing over towards the safe stored away in the closet, he retrieved his Glock 40 semiautomatic handgun. After checking the bathrooms, the other bedroom, and both balconies, Tre thought of the worst as there was still no sign of the love of his life. Pacing back and forth in the living room, he noticed a note on the table.

What the fuck is this he thought, examining the note.

The note read: What's up, baby boy. You don't know me but I know a lot about you. Well not a whole lot. But enough to have yo bitch. Yeah that's right. I got yo bitch and if you want to see this pretty face again then you will follow these instructions to the T. I want five million in cash and two hundred kilos by tomorrow. And if you need some help with the ransom, don't be shy to call her brothers. That won't be nothing to them, I heard they running shit in Miami. Oh yeah, NO POLICE!! I really shouldn't have to tell you that. Try any funny business and the bitch is dead.

P.S. Everybody have secrets, some never to be told and some come back to haunt you. Will be in touch soon :-).

After reading the ransom note, Tre's mind was racing.

"Who in the fuck will do this? And who knows about me way down here?" If the kidnappers were serious, he knew he had no time to waste.

"Damn, I don't have that kind of money or work. And how the fuck is I'm supposed to get in touch with her brothers. I don't know their fucking number. Fuck!" he snapped to himself just as his cell phone rang.

"Hello?" he answered on the first ring.

It was Lolita. "Tre, have you talked to Casina? I've been calling her for the past three hours. It's not like her not to call me."

"Lolita, I'm glad you called. You know how to get in touch with her brothers, right?" he asked, cutting her off.

"Yeah, why?"

"I can't explain right now, but tell them to get over to our condo asap," Tre said.

"Tre, you're scaring me. What's going on? Where's Casina?"

"Lolita, I need you to calm down and just contact her brothers. Time is against us," Tre ordered her, taking control of the situation. After hanging up, Tre sat back, trying to collect his thoughts.

*****

"Wake up, sleeping beauty!" Slow Juice said.

As Casina was coming out of a horrible nightmare, she tried to focus in front of her. But she couldn't. Her face was covered and she couldn't see the source of the voice. When she tried to move her hands and feet, she realized she was bound to a chair.

"What's going on?" Casina yelled, trying to free herself.

"Calm that shit down," Slow Juice barked.

"Who are you? Somebody help me! Please help!" Casina screamed at the top of her lungs.

"Are you finished now?" Slow Juice said. He wasn't worried about anybody hearing her cries. It was just that he was tired of hearing her yelling. They were in a secluded area on the outskirts of Miami, at his cousin Cochie's house. Slow Juice couldn't chance it at the star place located in the city's limits because of the risk factor.

"I see she's finally up," Star said as she entered the room. Turning in the direction of the voice, Casina tried to figure out where she had heard the voice before.

"Why are y'all doing this to me? Do y'all know who I am? Do y'all know the reputation of my brothers?" Casina said, trying to pump fear into their hearts.

"Speaking of your brothers, you better hope they and that boyfriend of yours come through. It would be a shame for your prettiness to go to waste," Slow Juice replied, now pumping fear into her.

"What have my brothers got me into? But they mention Tre also. What is this all about?" Casina thought to herself.

"What do y'all want from me?" she asked.

"I'm glad you asked. What's your cell phone number?" Slow Juice asked.

*****

Tre had everything a man could possibly want. Power. Money. Fame. But without Casina, none of that even mattered.

Sitting out on the balcony smoking, he heard banging at the door. Placing the blunt down, Tre walked over to the front door with his pistol in hand. Opening the door recklessly, he saw Casina's brothers standing before him.

Spotting the scar on Ricky's left cheek, Tre was able to tell them apart.

"Come in," he said, signaling them to enter.

Noticing Tre with a pistol in his hand, Rayman proceeded with caution and scanned his surroundings.

"What's so fucking important? Where's Casina at?" Ricky asked, taking notice of the mess in front of him.

Ignoring Ricky's comment, Tre closed the door and faced Rayman.

"Nigga, I know you hear me. If you had put yo hands on my sis, you're a dead man!" Ricky barked.

From the look on Tre's face, Rayman knew something was seriously wrong. "Tre, what's going on? Where's my little sis at?" he asked, hoping to hear something to comfort his suspicion.

Looking at the note in his hand, Tre passed it to Rayman.

"Did this nigga just pass you a piece of paper? What type of fuckboy shit you on? Nigga where the fuck is Casina?" Ricky yelled, ready to put his hands on Tre.

Signaling Ricky to calm down, Rayman read the note. After reading it, he dropped it. His whole world had just come crashing down on him. Just the thought of his little sister being held against her own will, God knows where, was killing him on the inside.

"Kidnap? Tre, what the fuck is going on?" Rayman shouted.

"What the fuck did you just say?" Ricky asked, not taking his eyes off Tre.

Through clenched teeth, Rayman snarled. "Tell me this ain't real."

"Oh hell no. I told you something was up with this nigga. He's trying to rob us! Where the fuck is my sister at, pussy!" Ricky shouted, pulling out his custom-made .45 and aiming it at Tre's head.

Like clockwork, Tre lifted his gun and aimed as well. "Nigga, this is yo second and the last time you'll be pulling a hammer out on me," he barked with vengeful eyes.

As the two stared each other down, Rayman studied Tre's demeanor. Either he was for real or he was a great actor. But either way, Rayman wasn't taking a chance. If someone had his sister, he wanted to get down to the bottom of it. But if by any chance Tre was behind this whole kidnap thing, he and everyone close to him would be as good as dead.

"Both of y'all need to put your fucking guns down. I'm getting sick of your shit, Ricky. Someone has our little sis and you want to play gangsta at a time like this?" Rayman snapped.

"Bro, I know you're not buying into this kidnap shit! He's after our money, I'm telling you," Ricky replied, his gun still trained on Tre.

"Nigga, I don't need yo money! I am money!" Tre said cockily.

"Ricky, look at him! Get a real good look! Now, do he really look like he's faking?" Rayman yelled.

"Bro, I don't trust him," Ricky responded.

"What other choice do we got?" Rayman said.

Looking Tre dead in the eyes, Ricky wanted him to know that he meant business before the words exited his mouth.

"If you're lying, you're a dead man," he said, lowering his gun.

"Yeah, whatever, nigga," Tre replied, showing no sign of fear.

"Now, who would do something like this?" Rayman asked Tre.

"That's what's fucking my head up. I don't know nobody down these parts and don't nobody know I'm down here," Tre replied.

"But someone do know you're here, and they know Casina is our sister," Rayman said. Just then, the ringing of a cell phone filled the air.

"You going to answer your cell phone?" Tre asked.

"That's not mine," Rayman replied, looking at Ricky.

Looking on the couch, Ricky noticed it was Casina's cell phone he had gotten her six months ago. Grabbing her phone, Ricky answered.

"Hello?"

"You got my money yet?" a male voice asked.

"Nigga, who this?!" Ricky shouted.

"The nigga that got yo bitch," came the reply.

"Nigga, you dead if you touch my sister!"

"O', so this is big bro talking. I'm glad y'all are all together," he replied.

Placing the cell phone onto speaker phone, Ricky continued to talk.

"Man, you know who you fucking with?"

"Listen, I don't give a fuck what you talking. You're in no position to be making any threats."

Looking at Ricky like he was crazy, Rayman signaled him to keep quiet.

"Listen here, this is her other brother. You have to give us time to come up with that kind of money and stuff," he said out loud.

"Ok, you have less than twenty-four hours," he replied, back to controlling the situation.

"How do I know my sister is okay?" Rayman asked.

There was a moment of silence.

"Hello," came Casina's voice.

"Casina!" Rayman yelled.

"Rayman, I--"

"Ok, ok, enough with that reunion shit. Have my money and my work on time," he barked, pulling the phone back from Casina.

"Listen, you will get what you want. But if you lay a single finger on my sister, I'll kill your whole fucking family," Rayman threatened.

"Good luck with that. I'll be in touch. Tick, tock, tick, tock, tick, tock," Slow Juice taunted before hanging up and destroying the SIM card.

CHAPTER 32: TIME IS AGAINST US

The three of them sat in the living room, trying to come up with solutions. The only thoughts that kept flushing their minds were of Casina and who was behind the kidnapping. Tre's brain was completely discombobulated. Everything that had transpired in the last forty-eight hours would have had any man on edge.

Rayman couldn't believe what was happening in their own city. Whoever was involved was either clueless as to who they were dealing with or they had a death wish. Rayman was going to keep his word, should anything happen to his sister. He would find them, kill them and their loved ones, and have God sort them out.

Ricky was upset as well; he wouldn't be able to forgive himself if something was to go wrong. The last time he and Casina were together, he had made a fool of himself and her. It may seem like he was hard on her at times but by all means he loved his sister. He just wasn't feeling this Tre guy; it was something about him...he just couldn't put his finger on it. If looks could kill, Tre would have been dead by how Ricky hawked him.

"Man, why the fuck are you looking at me like that? You got something on your mind, speak, nigga!" Tre barked. He was really fed up with Ricky's shit.

"You know what's on my fucking mind. How you got my sister into some bullshit."

"Me! Nigga, this shit happens in yo city. This shit would have never happened in Wilmington!"

"Fuckboy, that note said something about secrets. Maybe some shit that you did in the Carolina's done followed yo ass down here! That never crossed your mind now, did it?"

"First of all, it's Wilmington, Delaware, not Wilmington, North Carolina. Second, how the fuck would they know about y'all's operation. Maybe this is yo shit that got me and Casina into some bullshit," Tre said, flaring up. He was ready to place the paws on him.

"Did you just say Delaware?" Ricky asked, looking at his brother.

"Yeah! What, you fucking deaf now?" he replied, aggravated with all his questions.

"Not right now, Ricky," Rayman butted in, sensing where this conversation was going.

"But ain't this a coincidence, what if this --"

"Bro, leave that shit alone. We need to be focusing on Casina right now," Rayman reminded him, cutting him off. Ricky left it alone for now, but he wasn't dropping it. He was going to make a mental note about it and would address it later.

"Man, I'm not with this back-and-forth shit. What's our next move?" Tre asked, focusing himself back onto the love of his life.

"What you think? We're going to give them what they want. I'm not playing any games when it comes to my sister's life," Rayman said. He wanted that to be made clear.

"Well, I got a million, but I don't have any work," Tre said. If needed, he would hit Tommy and Nice up for some more money.

"I thought you was money," Ricky said sarcastically.

"Tre, keep your money. We can handle the ransom," Rayman commented, cutting his gaze to look at Ricky, not liking his statement.

"Fuck that, I'm about to put word out on the streets. These fuckboys don't know who they fucking with," Ricky barked.

"You do that, and we would have a hundred more niggas trying to get at us," Rayman told him.

"So, what the fuck you think is going to happen when we pay the ransom? You think it's going to stop there? This piece of shit could milk us dry," Ricky replied, making his point.

"So, Ricky, what you got on your mind, since you got it all figured out?" Rayman said.

"First, we need to holla at Dexter Boy and see if he could pinpoint where this number leads to. Just in case they call back, Dexter could track them; we might be dealing with some rookies. Next, we get the money and drugs together. We just need to hope Dexter Boy comes through; that way, we would have the upper hand on the situation," explained Ricky.

"Good thinking, bro, 'cause time is against us," Rayman replied, reaching for his cell phone and dialing Dexter Boy.

He had known Dexter Boy for years. Dexter Boy was one of those nerdy dudes who surfed the net all day and masturbated all night. He put the 'G' in genius. You'd think the IRS is bad, but you don't want no problems with Dexter Boy. After hanging up his call with Dexter Boy, Rayman heard a knock at the door. Simultaneously, the three of them aimed their guns at the door. Tre was the first to answer.

"Who is it?"

"It's me," Lolita replied from the other side of the door. Opening the door, Tre noticed she wasn't alone.

"My nig, what's going on?" C-low asked.

"They kidnapped Casina," Tre replied with hurt flashing in his eyes.

"What?!" Lolita screamed before fainting.

*****

Meanwhile on the outskirts of Miami, Slow Juice was enjoying a super head job from Star. If you think Super Head was a beast, Star was putting on a performance that would prove you wrong.

"Slurp! Smack! Slurp! Smack! Slurp! Slurp! Smack!"

"Goddamn, gurl, you have step yo shit up since I've been gone... Damn... Ssss... Shit!" he moaned, enjoying the special treatment he was receiving.

Casina couldn't believe her ears; they were getting their freak on right in front of her. She couldn't deny the fact that whoever the female was, was definitely doing the damn thing.

Why me, out of all people, why me? I know Tre is worried sick about me she thought as she began to say a silent prayer.

"Please, Father, save me from this evil. I know I haven't prayed since the death of my parents, Father. But I need your blessings now more than ever. I wasn't a bad person and I know I wasn't the perfect one either. But please don't let this be the end of my chapter, Father. Please help me out of this, in Jesus's precious name. Amen."

"Smack! Smack! Slurp! Slurp! Smack! Mmmm! Smack! Mmmm!"

Star was moaning with excitement as she took him in and out of her mouth like the pro she was. She smacked the tip of his head a few times on her lips before forcing it back into her warm zone.

"Oh shit, bitch, I'm about to cum," Slow Juice yelled. With just the tip of her lips, she sucked away while making popping sounds. Feeling his body tensing up, she really sucked him.
"Oh shit... Shit, stop, stop! Damn, girl!" Slow Juice cried, trying his best to get away from her locked jaws. Star had just sucked all his babies out of him, leaving his toes curled up in his boots.

"Y'all so nasty," Casina said, glad they were done.

"Awww, what, you felt left out?" Slow Juice said, pulling up his pants. Hearing someone opening the front door, Slow Juice reached for his gun and aimed it at the door. When he noticed it was Cochie, he lowered his gun.

"Damn, nigga, you was going to shoot me for coming into my own crib!"

"My fault, cuz," Slow Juice responded, fastening his belt buckle.

"Nigga, what type of freak shit you got going on up in my crib?" Cochie asked, looking at a Spanish female wiping her lips and the other one tied to his chair with his black pillow case over her heard.

"Slow your roll, cuz. Let me holla at you in the back for a second," Slow Juice replied, not allowing his cousin to say something stupid.

When Slow Juice and Cochie disappeared into the back, Star walked over to Casina.

"So, you like what you heard?" she said, rubbing her hands across Casina's breast.

"Bitch, don't touch me," Casina snapped, recoiling.

"I'll bet that man of yours would love my lips around his penis," Star taunted her.

"Whatever, my man would never mess with a slut like you," she assured her with attitude. Casina was certain now that she had heard that voice before. She just couldn't put a face to it. *I got to get this bitch to show me her face* "You talking a lot of shit for a person that don't want to be seen. I guess you scared," she said, hoping her plan would work.

"Scared? Bitch, ain't shit scared about me. You really want to know who I am?" Star said, reaching for the pillow case.
Casina could feel her tugging at the pillow case. Just as she had hoped, her plan was working.

"A', what the fuck you think you doing?" Slow Juice barked, entering back into the room.

"I -- I was just making sure she couldn't see, daddy," Star replied, scared to death.

"Bitch, sit yo ass down," Slow Juice ordered, not liking what he just saw.

Cochie walked in. After being informed of what was going on, Cochie was all for it. It was time to step his shit up anyways and claim his rightful spot in the drug game. Cochie stood 5' 10", one hundred and eighty-five pounds, dark-skin with a head full of dreadlocks. He was already making a couple of dollars, and with the proposition Slow Juice just gave him, it would easily place him over the hump.

208

"Where the fuck is them fools at with the food?" Slow Juice barked, referring to Trap and Peaches.

"I don't know, daddy, but could we finish what we started?" She wanted to get her thing off as well.

"I don't have time for that right now. I got to stay focused. It's too much a stake right now," he said.

"But, daddy," she whined.

Looking at Cochie, Slow Juice spoke.

"Cuz, handle that for me?" he said, referring to Star's horny ass.

"You don't have to tell me twice, cuz," he replied, leading Star towards his master bedroom.

That bitch is a nasty broad Casina thought.

Slow Juice was glad that Star was out of his hair. Grabbing his cell phone, he called Trap. Time was ticking and it was time to put his plan into full effect.

*****

Dexter Boy arrived a little over two hours later. They all sat in silence as he did what he did best.

Lolita was on the verge of having another nervous breakdown. She couldn't believe her best friend since preschool had been kidnapped. She remembered all the years growing up Casina was always there to protect her from danger. But now Casina was the one in danger and there wasn't anything she could do but sit and hope for the best.

"There, I'm finished. Everything is ready now. Once the kidnappers call Casina's cell phone back, we will be able to put a trace on it. But remember, when they call you have to keep them on the phone for at least a minute or so. That way I can pinpoint an accurate location on the signal," Dexter Boy instructed them.

"What about the range of the tracking device?" Ricky asked.

"You don't have to worry about that. I can track a mufucka from here to Hong Kong if I wanted to," Dexter Boy replied, feeling himself.

"Dexter Boy, you really don't know how much we needed you in on this one. Thanks," Rayman said.

"Any time. I've been doing business for the family all these years. Plus, Casina is like family to me too," he replied, but really he was thinking about all the nights he had masturbated just dreaming of being with Casina. Just the thought of her now was giving him an instant hard-on. Just then, they were interrupted by the ringing of a cell phone.

"That's Casina's cell phone," Lolita blurted out.

"I can see that, but it's a different number," Ricky informed them while looking at the screen.

"Man, give me the damn phone!" Rayman said, snatching it and answering it on the fourth ring. "Hello?"

"Tell me, you got my money and my shit?" Slow Juice said.

Recognizing the voice, Rayman snapped his fingers, signaling Dexter that it was the kidnapper on the phone.

"Keep him talking," Dexter Boy whispered, doing his thing.

"Is Casina okay?" Rayman asked, trying to buy himself some more time.

"Nigga, the bitch is fine! Do you got my shit?!"

Rayman was pissed as hell, but his sister's life was at stake so maintaining his cool was a must.

"Yeah, man, we got everything. We just trying to come up with the last million now," he assured him, trying to keep things cool.

"Well, you know how much time you have left. I will be in touch, tick...tock...tick...tock!" he replied before hanging up and destroying yet another SIM card.

"Wait! wait -- damn!" Rayman yelled. Facing Dexter Boy he spoke, "What we got?"

"Nothing, really. All I know is that the signal was strong in the Florida city area," Dexter Boy informed them.

"I'ma kill that fuckboy, him and this tick-tock shit is getting on my last nerves," Rayman said, getting frustrated. In the back of his mind, he was wondering who he knew from the Florida city area.

Out on the balcony, Tre and C-low were trying to collect their own personal thoughts. Overlooking the city, C-low thought he could get used to this kind of lifestyle. That was one of the main reasons why he had been coming down to Miami so much lately. Not to mention seeing Lolita's sexy behind in the process.

"My nig, this shit is too much, yo. And I appreciate you showing up at a time like this," Tre said.

"Man, listen, Tre. As soon as you told me what happened at the stash house, I said fuck this, I'm out of here too. I knew the heat would be coming eventually, so I bounced. I left the little homies with enough work, so if any fishy shit pops off, they know how to reach me. I'm just glad a nigga came down when he did."

"I'm glad too, homie," Tre replied.

"Now, let's go back in here and see what's up with yo girl."

As the two of them entered from the balcony, Ricky turned to their direction.

"Glad the two of you could finally join us. They got Casina somewhere in Florida city."

"Where the fuck is that at?" Tre asked.

It's towards the bottom of Florida," replied Rayman.

CHAPTER 33: SHE HAS TO BE INVOLVED

Things weren't sitting well with Tre; he was trying his hardest to find out who could pull something like this off. Who would come up in a place like this and kidnap a person without being seen?

Looking at Rayman, he spoke, "You know what, this shit ain't adding up. Yeah, the place was messed up, but there was no sign of forced entry. So how the fuck did they get in? How the fuck did they even get Casina out of here without being seen?"

"You right, that can only mean one of two things. One, she knew the person who came to the door or the kidnappers had a key to get in," Rayman said.

"Hold up! Fuck that, these muthafuckas have cameras here," Tre told them while heading towards the door.

"Slow down, playboy, we have to be careful. We don't want the police getting involved," Rayman said.

"They won't. I know what I'm doing," Tre replied.

"Well, hold up. I'm coming with you," Rayman said, heading out the door behind him.

They were downstairs and at the receptionist's desk in no time. Tre noticed there was another female standing behind the desk, one that he wasn't used to seeing.

"Excuse me, where's Selena at?" Tre asked, hoping she would be of some help.

"She called off for the rest of the day, but I'm filling in for her. Is there anything I could help you with?" she asked, eyeing Tre.

Tre saw how the receptionist was eyeing him like she was hungry and he was the main course. Without a doubt she was attractive; damn near every female in Miami was attractive. But this wasn't the time nor the place for that matter and he knew it.

"Yes, there is something you could help me with. I'm kind of in a little jam. I was just wondering if you could check to see if a package was delivered here earlier today," Tre asked with a charming look on his face.

"Yes, hold on, sir," she replied, blushing visibly. After checking the log sheet, she noticed that there wasn't anything there for any type of delivery.

"I'm sorry, sir, but I don't see anything on the log sheet. Is there anything else I could help you with?"

"Yeah, there is one more thing. Can you check the surveillance cameras from earlier?" Tre asked.

"Sir, I can get into some serious trouble for that," she informed him, tapping her index finger on the counter top.

"I understand that and by all means I would never want to put you in a position where it could cost you your job. But you know how these businesses are today. Everybody is trying to scam the next person out of something. And with me giving them my money up front, I think they're trying to pull a fast one on me," Tre replied, licking his lips and placing his hands on top of hers.

The touch of his hand made her pussy do the faucet drip.

"Okay, come this way, sir," she replied, leading them to a room in the back. The sign on the door read, "Employees Only." Once inside the small room, the receptionist walked over towards the section for the surveillance tapes.

"This is weird," she said with one hand on her hip and the other scratching her head.

"What's weird?" Tre asked with a concerned look on his face.

"The surveillance tapes are gone," she replied, still confused.

"And why would they be gone?" Rayman asked with a stern voice.

"Sir, I don't know. I'm new. They were here this morning when Selena trained me on how to check them," she told him.

"So, she would just leave a new trainee alone?" Rayman asked.

"When I went on break, she was here, and when I came back, she was gone. But she left a note saying that she was sick and to fill in for her. The head manager already left for the day. I hope she didn't get me into any trouble 'cause the guy from twenty-sixth floor complained too. He saw her on his floor and asked her if he had any mail or not and she never got back to him. Then I'm the one who's getting chewed out just like now," she replied nervously.

"No, sweetie, it's cool. Thanks for everything," Rayman said, passing her five crisp one-hundred dollar bills.

"Thank you so much," she replied, happy as hell.

Before heading back up the elevator, Rayman grabbed one of the business cards from off the front desk. On the front of it, it read, "Selena Jackson."

Rayman was starting to piece everything together: Tre was the mark and Casina was the key. But the kidnappers also knew about their operation as well. So maybe all of them were the marks and Casina was the key to their fortune. There was only one person so far that he thought could put the pieces together in this puzzle for him .

As he stuffed the business card in his pocket and headed up the elevator, he thought of that person: Selena Jackson.

*****

In a small neighborhood located in Carol City, Rayman and Tre sat outside, staring at Salina's home. After giving the business card to Dexter Boy, within minutes, Tre had found out everything there was to find out on Selena Jackson. He couldn't believe this bullshit was really happening.

The game had truly changed; you had to watch out for the people who knew you had money and also those who thought you had money. Tre didn't know which ones were the worse; people are always out to get something from someone. They say what goes around comes around. Tre and his crew got someone and now someone wanted what he had. But why was it that the innocent ones always got the bad end of the stick?

As the two sat scheming and puffing away, they both had their own thoughts of revenge. The smoke that clouded the truck wasn't the smoke of the sweet budded weed; the dark clouds were of angry and vengeful thoughts permeating the SUV. On the outside of the windshield, the world was still functioning. But inside, hell was forming as everything seemed to come to a standstill.

If Casina wasn't involved, Rayman could have handled things quite differently without a blink. But since she was, he had to handle things accordingly. 'Cause if anything was to go wrong, he would paint the streets red with the blood of his enemies.

Smoking weed really wasn't Rayman's thing; it was Ricky's forte. But with everything that had recently happened, it helped him ease his mind. Between the bullshit that happened to his parents and now Casina, he was on the verge of exploding at any moment.

After taking two more pulls, Rayman passed the blunt back to Tre.

"Man, you ready? 'Cause if anything should happen to my little sis, it's on," he said, his head low but his eyes looking straight forward.

"She's going to be alright, man. I thought we was going to wait," Tre replied as he exhaled the sweet bud.

"Fuck that shit, time is not on our side, remember?" he remarked, clenching his fist.

"You right, fuck it. Let's go," Tre said, moving for the door handle. As the two exited the vehicle, their adrenaline was running amok. Neither of them cared about their surroundings as they approached the home. Noticing there was no entry point from the front, they proceeded towards the back of the house. Once around back, Tre was the first to notice that the window over what seemed to be the kitchen area was slightly open.

"That's where we can enter at," Tre said, pointing towards the window.

"Well, lead the way, Spiderman," Rayman teased.

"Ha, ha, very funny," he replied, proceeding through the kitchen window. Once inside, Tre did a quick sweep of the area before sticking his head back out the window.

"Man, the coast is clear, yo."

"Okay, open the door then. I ain't climbing through no window," Rayman said, peeking around. The weed was beginning to make him paranoid.

"Man, what if the alarm sets off?" Tre stated.

"Man, I stopped in the front when we walked up. There wasn't no sign of any type of alarm systems. Hurry up before someone sees us," Rayman replied.

Inside the house, they both went their separate ways, sweeping every inch of the home for clues. Rayman went upstairs while Tre went downstairs. While searching through the bedrooms, Rayman realized Selena was a natural born freak as he looked around the master bedroom. The room had all sorts of different sized and colored dildos displayed. All different flavors of motion lotion were there too. It looked like a porn shop.

"I know this bitch ain't putting all that up in her," Rayman thought to himself, referring to the eighteen-inch dildo displayed in front of him.

Downstairs, Tre was getting frustrated. After forty-five minutes of searching, they both came up empty-handed.

"Man, you find anything?" Rayman asked, walking up to Tre.

"Nah, how about you?" Tre replied.

"Shit, all I found was a camera," Rayman said.

"Well, what's on it?"

"I don't know. I'm about to check now," he said, turning it on.

"What the fuck!" Rayman said with a screwed-up face as he scrolled through the pictures.

"What is it?"

"This bitch is a freak for real. All I see is pictures of different types of dicks. Hold up, it's a few pictures of you and Casina in here."

Looking at the pictures, Tre could clearly see they were taken the night of Casina's birthday.

"So that bitch was scoping us out, but why?" he asked.

"Come on now, Tre, you look like money. She wasn't stupid, she could smell money all over you. Then look where y'all was staying at: the Akoya. That shit is expensive to stay up in," he schooled him.

"Man, that bitch is a dead bitch," Tre snapped, ready to fuck something up.

"In due time, but for now we have to bounce. 'Cause if she is really involved, I don't think she's stupid enough to come back here."

"Cool, but we're going out the front door this time," Tre said.

"Why, you don't like windows no more?" Rayman joked.

"Whatever, nigga," he replied back as they walked out the front door.

Rayman was starting to like Tre. Plus, if his sister was truly in love with him, he didn't want to come between their love. He would just have to convince Ricky to look at it from his point of view.

Outside, Star couldn't believe what she was seeing. She sat in awe as she watched the two emerge from her home. Once they were in their vehicle and out of sight, she picked up her cell phone and dialed Slow Juice.

"Fuck! How did they find me? Slow Juice is going to be pissed," she spat as she waited for him to answer.

CHAPTER 34: STOP PLAYING WITH MY INTELLIGENCE

Slow Juice was waiting patiently for Star's arrival. He couldn't believe she was that careless. First, he caught her about to reveal herself to Casina, and now this. It was too much on the line for her to be making careless mistakes like that. Death and prison weren't an option for him right now, and he was going to make sure of that.

Out in the front room, Cochie was surfing the net when Star came strolling in. The look Peaches gave her was enough info to let her know she was in deep shit. After a quick survey of the room, Star noticed Slow Juice wasn't present.

"Where's he at?" Star asked with a perplexed look on her face.

Nobody responded. Instead, they both pointed towards the back bedroom.

A lump formed quickly in the back of her throat. The walk down the hall felt like the walk many took down death row. The closer she got to the room, the more fear overcame her. It was as if a judgment cloud hovered over her. She felt like turning around and running out of the house. But she knew it wouldn't be long before Slow Juice would hunt her down and probably kill her for running.

Just before she was about to knock on the door Slow Juice's voice traveled from the other side ordering her to come in.

"How the fuck he know I was standing here?" she thought to herself before entering the room of doom.

Sitting on the edge of the bed, Slow Juice was drinking a cup of coffee, a habit he had picked up from doing prison time. The mysterious look he gave her sent chills of fear down her spine. It was as if he could see right through her.

"Daddy, I can ex--"

But before she could finish, he placed his finger to his lips to silence her. Once his coffee was finished, he placed it down on the nightstand and rose from the bed. As he unbuttoned his pants, he hawked Star before freeing his limp penis.

"You just going to stand there?" he asked, now stroking his manhood.

Scared, but turned on at the same time, Star dropped to her knees in no time to perform the best blow job ever. After raising him to his maximum length, Slow Juice turned her around and ripped off her shorts, literally tearing them to shreds.

Ramming his penis into her pussy like a wild man, he sent a sharp pain through her.

"Ahhhhhhhhh!" she cried out.

Ignoring her cries, he continued to devour her insides. Since her pussy was known to many as 'The Gusher,' the pain soon turned into pleasure as she threw it back like a professional, matching stroke for stroke. Thinking things were at its worst, Star was enjoying her punishment as Slow Juice continued to pound away. All you could hear was ass smacking and loud grunting sounds.

"Yes, daddy, fuck this pussy! Oh shit, that's my spot! I've been a bad girl!!! Oh shit, I'm about to cum!!" she yelled, biting down on her bottom lip.

Grabbing a handful of her hair, Slow Juice slowly grabbed his pistol from in between the bed. Caught up in the moment, Star never saw it coming as the bullet exited the front of her forehead. Still pounding away, he shot warm, sticky semen deep into her pussy. Within seconds, Cochie, Peaches, and Trap came busting into the room.

"Is everything cool, cuz?" Cochie was the first to speak.

"It is now, you feel me," Slow Juice replied, wiping off his dick with the bed sheets.

Seeing Star lying lifeless like that in a growing pool of blood let Peaches know not to cross Slow Juice.

"You want me to feed her to the alligators out back?" Cochie suggested.

"Yeah, but first, I need to send a message, you feel me. Do you by any chance have a machete?" Slow Juice asked, a grin on his face.

*****

"Are all the tracking devices stashed properly?" Dexter Boy asked, thinking sexual thoughts of Casina. If Tre, Ricky, or Rayman only knew half of his dirty thoughts, he would be dead right where he stood.

"Yeah, we placing the last one in now," Ricky replied, wrapping up the last kilo.

Out of the two hundred kilos, there were five state-of-the-art tracking devices stashed among them. So wherever the

223

cocaine went, they would have an accurate location, thanks to Dexter Boy.

"Man, that shit must be some Grade A shit, 'cause it got my hands numb as shit," Tre said, getting up to wash his hands.

"Rookie, I told you to wear gloves. I can tell you never dealt with no real weight before," Ricky bragged with his chest poked out.

"Don't get it fucked up, I'm far from a slouch. If I had a major connect, sky's the limit. My area is a gold mine," Tre replied, making clear his position in the drug game.

"The two of y'all act like y'all brothers or som'em. The way y'all be arguing, let me find out," Rayman said, but also making a mental note of what Tre had just said.

"Yeah, whatever," Ricky replied, not liking the sound of that.

On the couch, C-low was comforting Lolita through this tragic situation. Never would she have thought something like this would happen. She kept playing all the possibilities over and over again in her head.

"Baby, once y'all get Casina back, I don't think I can live here anymore. I just don't feel safe. What if something like that should happen to me?" Lolita wondered, giving C-low the puppy eyes.

"Lolita, don't talk like that. I would never let nothing like that happen to you as long as I'm around," he assured her, rubbing his hands down the side of her face.

"You sure, baby?"

"You got my word, mami," he replied, sincerely.

"Well, the money is counted, and the work is straight. So, all we have to do is wait for them to call," Dexter Boy said.

"We have a few more hours left. So they will probably call between now and then," Rayman added.

What they heard next had them all on alert.

"Knock! Knock! Knock!"

"Who is it?" Tre yelled while walking towards the door with his pistol in hand.

"You have a delivery, sir," a female voice spoke from the other side of the door.

Peeping through the peephole, Tre was at ease when he saw it was the same young lady from yesterday with a big box in her hand. After tucking his pistol, he signaled the rest of them to do the same before opening the door. The fragrance she was wearing was astonishingly refreshing, as if she had just put it on.

"Here you go, sir. I guess they weren't trying to scam you after all. Your name's not on it, but it says to deliver to this address. I wanted to personally deliver it to you so that there wouldn't be any problem," the receptionist said, passing Tre the big box.

After scanning the box, Tre noticed it had a small smiley face on it just like the smiley face he had seen on the kidnapper's ransom note.

"Did you by any chance see who gave this to you?" Tre asked.

"No, sir. Andrew, the valet, brought it to me. He said a lady dropped it off and asked for it to be delivered to this address. Is there a problem?" she asked, hoping it wasn't.

"No, everything is fine. Just was curious, that's all," he assured her. Digging into his pants pockets, Tre pulled out two one-hundred dollar bills and passed it to her to show his appreciation.

"Thank you, sir," she said, strolling away happier than a kid at a candy store. She could get used to this job; at the rate the customers were paying her, she could easily retire at a young age. She would have to tell her best friend about this job, 'cause once again, Selena hadn't shown up for work. No call, no show. After shutting the door, Tre sat the box on the counter wondering what was in it.

"I know it's from the kidnappers, but what do you think is in it?" he asked, breaking the silence between them.

"The fuck if we know. Open it and see," Ricky stated.

"What if it's a bomb or something?" Dexter Boy blurted out, with a worried look on his face.

"I really doubt that, Dexter Boy. It's a kidnapping, not an assassination attempt," Rayman replied, making a whole lot of sense.

"Yeah, good point. I'm tripping," he said, feeling stupid.

As Tre tore away the top of the box, a foul odor crept up to his face. After removing the thick styrofoam from the top of the box, Tre was shocked at what he saw. He pushed the box out of his hands, causing a head to tumble out of the box onto the marble floor. Seeing the sight of a head without a body caused a few to panic.

"Damn, you act like you never seen a head before," Ricky said to Tre, grabbing the head by the hair.

"I seen plenty of heads in my days, but they're usually attached to the body," he replied, gaining his composure.

Tre realized the head belonged to Selena.

"That's Selena Jackson right there!" Tre told them.

"What?" Rayman said, with a puzzled look.

"This fell out of the box," Tre said, bending down and picking up what he believed to be a note.

"It's a note from them again," he said before reading the note aloud.

"I believe this is what y'all been searching for. I hope you can get some answers out of her now. Ha, ha, ha, oh yeah, you're riding on thin ice. Now stop playing with my intelligence. Tick, tock, tick, tock, tick, tock. :)"

"How the fuck did they know?" Tre shouted, passing around the note.

"I think we're dealing with a professional," Dexter Boy suggested.

"He ain't no professional. He's just on top of his game," Ricky said.

"Well, whatever he is, we need to be careful from here on out, 'cause that could have easily been Casina in that box," Rayman said, looking at them with a serious look.

"You right, bro. We need to get more focused," he added.

"Yeah, and start by getting rid of that fucking head," he ordered Ricky who was still holding the head in his hand. Tre had a distressed look on his face; all the drama was beginning to take a toll on him.

"A' Tre, let me holla at you, homie," C-low said.

Walking over to C-low, Tre spoke, "What's good?"

"You Tre, you need some rest. You haven't stopped moving since shit went down back home. We're going to need you on full alert when shit goes down," C-low told him.

"You right, I just miss her. But I'm going to take a quick nap. If anything jumps off, wake me up asap," Tre replied.

"I got you, homie," C-low said as Tre walked off towards the back room.

CHAPTER 35: THE EXCHANGE

The upper atmosphere was taking on an apricot tint as the two vehicles pulled into the warehouse parking lot. Ricky and Rayman's car's brake lights lit up as Tre and C-low pulled alongside them. The warehouse seemed to be abandoned and from the looks on the outside, it had been abandoned for quite some time.

Tre peered over at Ricky and Rayman.

"So what now?" Just then, two large metal doors groaned. Someone came into view as the gates opened. The figure was cloaked by a black mask. It waved them to enter.

"I guess we're about to see," Rayman said.

Rayman and Ricky drove into the warehouse with Tre and C-low tailing close behind. The inside was much bigger than what it appeared from the outside. A black minivan with tinted windows sat midway in the warehouse. They stopped a few yards from it. The minivan's driver side door opened and a man hopped out, armed with an automatic rifle.

Tre, C-low, Raymond, and Ricky were all now standing outside their vehicles. Four duffle bags sat in front of them. Ricky's legs were planted wide.

"Where the fuck is my sister!" he barked.

Just then, the side door of the van slid open. Two more masked men, armed to the teeth, emerged. One reached back in, grabbing hold of Casina by the arm and forcefully pulling her from the van.

"Come on, bitch!" he yelled, pointing the pistol to the back of her head.

Tre, C-low, Ricky, and Rayman looked on in anger as they walked towards them, stopping halfway. Casina looked like she'd been crying for hours. The sight of her presence made them even more pissed off.

"Casina, you okay?" Rayman shouted.

With duct tape over her mouth and her hands tied in front of her, all she could do was nod her head up and down.

"Mothafuckas!" Tre yelled, ready to kill them all. It hurt him to see the woman he loved in a situation like this.

"Nigga, you better calm down and remember who's in control," the kidnapper with the automatic rifle warned him.

"You know you're a dead man, right?" Rayman said.

"Yeah, yeah, you said that already," he replied, now leveling his riffle on him. He then signaled the short, masked man to grab the duffle bags. Looking at his cousin, he signaled him over.

"Check that shit, make sure the money and the drugs is straight," he ordered.

"Fuckboy, you got what you wanted, now hand over my sister!" Ricky spat.

"Patience, my friend," the one in-charge replied.

"Money look like it's here, boss," he said, moving towards the other two duffle bags. After searching through both bags, he looked up.

"Yeah, and the work is counted for."

"Nice doing business with y'all. Maybe we can do more in the near future," he smiled, signaling his partner to release Casina.

He freed her hands and kicked her in the ass. Casina lost her balance and hit the ground hard. Seeing that, the leader knew it was on. Tre was the first one to react, sending four shots into the kidnapper's upper body, sending him flying backwards. The other kidnapper aimed at Ricky and Rayman as his handgun came to life.

Bullets flew everywhere; it looked like a war zone. Using the van door as a shield, the leader let his rifle do what it do best. Destroy. Everybody took cover, still exchanging fire.

"Let's go," the leader yelled. Once they were all in the van, the leader drove straight through the rotten doors, which fell to their sides upon impact, while the others hung out by the van, still firing away.

C-low was still shooting until they were out of sight. Hearing the cries of Casina made him turn around in her direction.

"No! Please God, no! Tre, wake up, baby! Get up! Tre!" she cried out.

Walking towards her side, C-low knew his homie was gone. Ricky and Rayman watched in silence as their sister mourned. Even C-low shed a few tears.

"Come on, Casina. We have to go," C-low said.

"No! I am not leaving him! C-low, he can't be dead, he's going to be a father!" she yelled, holding the lower part of her belly.

*****

"Casina!" Tre woke up screaming.

"Calm down, homie, it was just a dream," C-low said.

"A dream?" Tre replied as he looked around and noticed he was still inside the condo.

"Yeah, homie, a dream," C-low assured him.

"Damn, I thought I lost her. It just felt so real," Tre said, wiping the beads of sweat from his forehead.

"Well, it's on, they just called. Showtime. Let's go and get Casina back," C-low replied before walking out.

Three and a half hours later, pulling up to the warehouse, Ricky and Rayman parked while C-low and Tre pulled alongside them.

Damn, this is how the dream started off Tre thought while observing his surroundings.

"A' homie, if anything should happen to me, make sure Casina makes it out alive."

"Man, everything is going to be cool. We're going to get your girl back and then deal with them fools later. Remember, Dexter Boy is going to know their every move," C-low assured him.

"Man, I want to thank you for all of this. You don't have to be here," Tre said.

"Man, save all that shit, and let's get your girl back. Then you can thank me later."

The four of them stared at the abandoned warehouse. The warehouse was decrepit and old. Rusty gates were leaning into each other as in sorrowful consolation. But there was no such sort of emotion in either one of those in the cars.

They all sought retaliation in full measure. Neither one of them knew what to expect once they entered the warehouse, and they did not know exactly how it would all end.   But one thing they did know was certain and true....

Casina's life was at stake.

TO BE CONTINUED....

So Real You Feel You've Lived It!

1. DO THEY GET CASINA BACK?

2. WHAT HAPPENS WITH CREAM AND NICE?

3. WHATEVER HAPPENS TO SHERRY?

4. DO TRE AND NICE SETTLE THEIR DIFFERENCES?

5. DOES DETECTIVE O'NEAL BRINGS DOWN THE TNT CREW ONCE AND FOR ALL?

6. DO RICKY AND RAYMAN EVER FIND OUT ABOUT TRE'S SECRETS?

THESE ARE THE QUESTIONS THAT CAN ONLY BE ANSWERED IN *STREET VICTIMS II (THE STAKES ARE HIGH)*

COMING SOON....

THANKS FOR SUPPORTING MY BOOK! YOU'LL LOVE THE NEXT ONE EVEN MORE!

Street Knowledge Publishing LLC
1902-B Maryland Ave
Wilmington, DE 19805
TOLL FREE: **1.888.401.1114**
www.streetknowledgepublishing.com

Date: _____

Purchaser _____

Mailing Address _____

City _____ State _____ Zip Code _____

Qty.	ISB Number	Title of Book	Price Each	Total
	978-0-9822515-6-0	Bloody Money	$15.00	
	978-0-9822515-9-1	Bloody Money 2	$15.00	
	978-0-9799556-4-8	Bloody Money 3	$15.00	
	978-0-9799556-0-0	Tommy Good story	$15.00	
	978-0-9822515-0-8	Tommy Good Story II	$15.00	
	978-0-9746199-1-0	Me & My Girls	$15.00	
	978-0-9746199-0-3	Cash Ave	$15.00	
	978-0-9822515-1-5	Merry F$$kin' Xmas	$15.00	
	978-0-9799556-0-7	A Day After Forever	$15.00	
	978-0-9822515-3-9	A Day After Forever 2	$15.00	
	978-0-9746199-6-5	Don't Mix the Bitter with the Sweet	$15.00	
	978-0-9799556-9-3	Playing For Keeps	$15.00	
	978-0-9799556-3-1	Pain Freak	$15.00	
	978-0-9799556-5-5	Dipped Up	$15.00	
	978-0-9799556-6-2	No Love No Pain	$15.00	
	978-0-9746199-4-1	Dopesick	$15.00	
	978-0-9799556-7-9	Lust, Love & Lies	$15.00	
	978-0-9746199-7-2	The Queen of New York	$15.00	
	978-0-9746199-8-9	Sin 4 Life	$15.00	
	978-0-9822515-4-6	A Little More Sin	$15.00	
	978-0-9746199-5-8	The Hunger	$15.00	
	978-0-9746199-3-4	Money Grip	$15.00	
	978-0-9822515-7-7	Young Rich and Dangerous	$15.00	
	978-1-944151-26-3	Street Victims	$15.00	
	978-1-944151-28-7	Street Victims II	$15.00	
	978-1-944151-30-3	Street Victimes III	$15.00	
	978-1-944151-32-4	A Small Wonder	$15.00	
	978-1-944151-45-4	Coup De Grace	$15.00	
	978-1-944151-47-8	Burton Boys (May 2017)	$15.00	
	978-1-944151-56-0	Burton Boys 2	$15.00	
	978-1-944151-58-4	Burton Boys 3	$15.00	
	978-1-944151-00-3	Dirty Living	$15.00	
	978-1-944151-65-2	Watch What You Say	$15.00	
		Total Books Ordered	Quantity	
			Subtotal	

SHIPPING/HANDLING (Via U.S. Priority Mail)	
$7.20 for 1st book, $2.00 for each additional book	
Institutional Check & Money Orders ONLY	Shipping
(No Personal Checks Accepted)	Total

Total $

Street Knowledge Publishing LLC
1902-B Maryland Ave
Wilmington, DE 19805
TOLL FREE: **1.888.401.1114**
www.streetknowledgepublishing.com

Date: _____

Purchaser _____

Mailing Address _____

City _____ State _____ Zip Code _____

Qty.	ISB Number	Title of Book	Author	Price Each	Total
	Butterfly Collection				
		Beautiful Demise	K.D. Harris	$13.99	
		Scarred	K.D. Harris	$13.99	
		Pressure (Coming April 2017)	K.D. Harris	$13.99	
		Dying to Fit In (Coming June 2017)	K.D. Harris	$13.99	
		Legacy (Coming August 2017)	K.D. Harris	$13.99	
		Classy Clique (Coming Sept. 2017)	K.D. Harris	$13.99	
		Caged Secrets (Coming Nov. 2017)	K.D. Harris	$13.99	
		Messy Media (Coming Dec. 2017)	K.D. Harris	$13.99	
	SKP Erotica				
	978-1-944151-04-1	Beyond Measure	K.D. Harris	$15.00	
	978-1-944151-06-5	Beyond Measure II	K.D. Harris	$15.00	
	978-1-944151-62-1	Beyond Measure III (April 2017)	K.D. Harris	$15.00	
	978-1-944151-08-9	The Games We Play	K.D. Harris	$15.00	
	978-1-944151-02-7	For The Love Of It	K.D. Harris	$15.00	
	Eric B Crime Novels				
	978-1-944151-20-1	That Was Dirty	Wasiim	$15.00	
	978-1-944151-22-5	It Gets Dirtier	Wasiim	$15.00	
	978-1-944151-24-9	As Dirty As It Gets	Wasiim	$15.00	
	978-0-9799556-8-6	Money and Murder	Fred Brown	$15.00	
	978-1-944151-35-5	Money and Murder II	Fred Brown	$15.00	
	978-1-944151-39-7	Money and Murder III	Fred Brown	$15.00	
	978-1-944151-49-2	Scandalous Ties	Jermaine "Ski" Buchanan	$15.00	
	978-1-944151-51-5	Scandalous Ties II	Jermaine "Ski" Buchanan	$15.00	
	978-1-944151-52-2	Scandalous Ties III	Jermaine "Ski" Buchanan	$15.00	
	978-1-944151-55-3	Scandalous Ties IV	Jermaine "Ski" Buchanan	$15.00	
	978-0-9799556-2-4	Courts in the Streets	Kevin Bullock	$15.00	
	978-0-9822515-5-3	Courts in the Streets II	Kevin Bullock	$15.00	
	978-1-944151-43-0	Courts in the Streets III	Kevin Bullock	$15.00	
		Total Books Ordered		Quantity	
				Subtotal	
SHIPPING/HANDLING (Via U.S. Priority Mail) $7.20 for 1st book, $2.00 for each additional book Institutional Check & Money Orders ONLY (No Personal Checks Accepted)				Shipping Total	
		Total		$